Festival in the Park

Festival in the Park

by HELEN COPELAND

Illustrated by HAROLD BERSON

CROWN PUBLISHERS, INC.   NEW YORK

To Dad and Ruthie, with love

Contents

The Shortcut

Duncan McKenna was blasted out of sleep at four A.M. when his alarm clock went off. He reached to the table beside his bed and mashed the cutoff button flat. In the bathroom he dressed quickly, climbed out the window, and slid down the rope tied to a pine-tree limb, an easy reach from the back of the house. His bicycle was where he had left it, leaning against a tree in the front yard.

It was only a matter of minutes after the blare of that buzzer, and here he was streaking along under the street lights in the predawn darkness of this Sunday morning in September, heading toward the country with his friend Louie. This was his first day of helping Louie deliver the Sunday *Charlotte Observer*. The wire saddlebag baskets that straddled his back fender were stuffed to bulging with papers. Louie did the weekday route before school alone, but Sunday's load, he said, was "impossibly monstrous," and that was the only reason he had asked Duncan to help. For his part in it, Duncan was to receive a dollar a Sunday.

He stopped in front of a red brick house crawling with ivy, supported the bike on its stand, pulled out a newspaper, and laid it on the rubber doormat. From across the street Louie called softly, "Hey, Dunc, collect from the one on the corner, the yellow brick." In the early morning damp under the trees, his voice sounded too loud, like whispers booming out in an empty auditorium.

In the black iron mailbox of the yellow brick house Duncan found an envelope with money in it. There would be four such collections to make on his side of the street. Louie considered these cash customers a nuisance.

Out near the end of the route the houses and street lights were farther apart. Panting from the long uphill climb, Duncan realized what a big job Louie had taken on, delivering this whole route by himself every day before school and on Saturdays. The Sunday deal with Duncan was really generous too. In addition to the dollar he was paying Duncan, Louie had promised free labor whenever Duncan needed help in his backyard project—a waterfall and pool to be built for fish and "critters," Louie's name for all the amphibious creatures that Duncan had a habit of finding and keeping.

Duncan visualized that waterfall as he coasted down a hill with the wet spray whistling off his tires.

It would be a pyramid-shaped tower of rocks about as tall as Monroe, Duncan's small fifth-grade friend. From the top of it water would spew forth and trickle down to a pool below. What a way to display his rock collection!

After every summer vacation trip with his father and mother, the rock pile in Duncan's backyard behind the gardenia bush had grown until now rocks from every state in the Union were stacked up deep and dusty under a layer of pine needles.

The pool, which was to be edged with rocks, was a necessary part of his science project. It would be the training arena for a huge soft-shelled turtle. Sixth graders were allowed to enter the Junior High Science Fair if their teachers okayed the idea. Miss Frazer had already given her approval for what Duncan said would be "The Pacification of Trionyx Spiniferus and a Comparison of Reptile IQ with That of Rodents." His father had helped him think up that title. Duncan's father was the director of the Charlotte Nature Museum. He was used to helping kids with their science projects. To Duncan's knowledge never before had anyone tested the intelligence of a soft-shelled turtle. His turtle was going to be so tame it would eat out of his hand.

But right now, since the pool hadn't yet been built, this not-yet-famous turtle, as big as a giant-sized pizza, was hiding angrily under the sand in a twenty-gallon tank. Having been caught only yesterday on a picnic at Lake Wylie, it was totally uncivilized. The thrill of the capture came back as Duncan pedaled into the curving driveway of a large white-pillared house. He had been walking along in the shallow water, looking for crayfish for his pet raccoon, Tony, when under one foot the sand began to shiver. Nothing but a soft-shell burrowing in could have caused that queer little earthquake! With his foot firmly planted, he dug down on both sides, hoping of course to connect with the leathery sides and not the dangerous front and tail. Yes, he had the sides, and he brought it up frantic, with all four feet flailing the air. Duncan's wrists were soundly spanked by long flaps of dead skin that trailed off the turtle's webbed feet. But the danger was in the unbelievably long neck. You had to know where to grab to be safe from the reach of the bony jaws. Duncan left a paper on the welcome mat and got back on his bicycle grinning as he thought of the fun he'd have scaring Louie with the turtle. Louie, he was sure, had never seen anything like it before.

Louie was not a naturalist. He had come only last year to Charlotte from a big city where apparently the only kind of "critter" he had ever looked at, eyeball to eyeball, was a parakeet, which had lived in a cage in the lobby of his apartment house.

Duncan, on the other hand, had grown up here in Charlotte, North Carolina, near Freedom Park and the Nature Museum where his father was in charge of things. Duncan had a way with animals,

and had tamed many different kinds for the animal-handling classes at the museum. But, to tame a soft-shell . . . what a project! He wouldn't tell Miss Frazer what biters soft-shells were, or she might take back her approval.

Louie was waiting at the end of the paper route, pretending to be asleep as he leaned on his bicycle against an elm tree. His long legs were cocked up on the handlebars; his shaggy head drooped; his face puffed and flopped as he snored raggedly.

Duncan gave the rear fender a slap. "Wake up, you nut."

Louie came to with a rubbery grin; then he abruptly scowled. "Hope you didn't run over any newly seeded lawns or squash any flowers. I get docked twenty-five cents a complaint." He looked up at the street light. "Gosh, we're through early. I'm starved. Let's go back by the doughnut place at the shopping center. It stays open all night."

Pink streaks fingered up into the misty gray sky as the boys rode on beyond houses and sidewalks. Some black and white cows, indistinct in the fog, were lying down in a pasture, but birds were awake and chirping. A well-packed dirt path angled off from the road through an open field grown over with weeds.

Duncan circled his bike around in the street. "Is that a shortcut, Louie?"

Louie came back and looked up the path. It went out of sight at the top of a hill. "Could be. Can't see where it goes, but it might be the way the country kids get to Eastover School. It might come out at the shopping center. Let's see if it does. I can sure smell those doughnuts!"

The solid dirt path was wide enough for Duncan and Louie to ride their bicycles two abreast. At the top of the rise, beyond which they hadn't been able to see from Randolph Road, they got off their bikes to stare downhill at a broad, treeless expanse grown up in brambles and brittle goldenrod. A winding creek with high banks snaked across the land. And almost hidden in the fog was a monumental iron truss bridge, straddling the creek at such a slant that it seemed about to topple from its moorings.

Duncan caught his breath and pointed. "Do you see what I see?"

"Ye gods," Louie whispered back. "A ghost bridge!"

Duncan nodded. "It's been dead a long time too."

Apparently in the old days, before the Duke Power Company built dams, floods had overflowed the creek banks, eroding the ground under the bridge till its supports gave way. Now its tall black beams resembled the masts and spars of a sailing ship that had run aground on a reef.

"Poor cockeyed bridge," Louie said sadly. "I'd rather see it get blasted by lightning than just totter over in the creek."

"Maybe it's still used though, Louie. This path has to get over the creek somehow, if it's heading for Eastover school and the shopping center. The *old* Randolph Road must have gone over that bridge. Maybe the path joins the old road."

Slowly they walked their bikes down the hill until the dirt path was intersected by the cracked remains of an old tar road. Yes, it was surely old Randolph Road. Beyond the creek was a little more pasture-land and then a black wall of trees.

Duncan strained to see through the semidarkness. "It goes across the bridge, I think, but I can't see any break in those woods where a path could get through."

"It wouldn't stop here though, Dunc." Louie pushed his bicycle up onto the tar road. "What's there here for anyone to beat a path to?"

To the right the road was fuzzy with weeds sprouting up through the cracks in the tar. Obviously whoever came this way always walked to the left across the bridge.

Louie gazed forlornly up at the rusty upper beams of the doomed bridge. "Poor bridge," he sighed. To Louie, who planned to be a great industrial artist someday, bridges and buildings had personalities. But suddenly Louie came out of his daydream; he shot a startled glance at Duncan. "I smell some-thing!" he said, sniffing the air. Duncan smelled it too—a breeze from across the creek, ripe with the odor of dung. "Come on, Dunc, let's get out of here. We must of dead-ended at a pigpen."

"It's not pigs, Louie."

"Well, it's no smell of doughnuts wafting through the trees. Let's beat it. This is no shortcut to East-over." Louie began to turn his bicycle around.

"Just a minute, Louie. Let's find out what smells so bad. It's sure to be some sort of animal."

"That's what I'm afraid of," Louie said. But he laid his bicycle down, and silently on rubber soles followed Duncan toward the dilapidated bridge.

The Old Man
and the Dogs

To board the listing deck of the bridge, they had to step over a chasm between the road and the bridge. Through this crack they could see down to a slow stream of water that caught a little of the rosy sky in its mirror surface.

A breeze rank with the smell of manure drifted up from the direction of the dense pinewoods. Louie grabbed his nose. "Look, Dunc, ol' buddy, I'd rather not stumble into a pig, you know, or a whole gang of pigs in the dark. With fangs. I've seen 'em with fangs in the *National Geographic*. They hunt in packs like wolves. Tear you apart. They're heavy sleepers till you're right up on 'em."

"Wolves don't hunt people. That's just a superstition."

"I'm not talking about wolves."

"You said it, though."

"But it's pigs I smell."

"It's not pigs, Louie. I know how they smell. Anyway they'd be in a pen, so come on. Hey! Look down there, a shack!"

Louie leaned over the rusty railing of the bridge to look where Duncan pointed—across the creek and down, almost under the bridge. Nestled close to one of the concrete bridge supports was a small tar-paper–roofed shack. A high bushy bank screened it from the road.

"Neat," Louie said. "I bet some kids built it."

It was made almost completely of old doors. It was hard to tell which was the working door. A stack of kindling and a pile of coal lay between the shack and the bushy bank; above the firewood a stovepipe elbowed out. Only one of the doors that they could see had windows in it—two dinky peep-holes so high up you'd have to be a giant to see out of them. They glistened in the opaque pink light like eyes glowering out from under the overhanging roof. In front of the shack was a bare yard and a path that curved around and apparently went up the bushy bank to join the tar road. What went on here? Duncan wondered. The well-traveled path, the smell of fresh manure . . .

He squinted into the dim light and finally found what he was looking for. "Look, Louie," he whispered, pointing down the creek. "In there among those trees. I think that's a pen with animals in it."

"Oh, my gosh, what kind?"

Vaguely distinguishable among the dark trees was a wire enclosure, and inside it were twenty or so ghostly forms, little and big, lying down on the ground. "Your 'pigs,' Louie."

"They're not pigs, Dunc. They're goats. Goats are known to be stinkers. But they're asleep. Let's don't disturb them or they'll get up and baa at us."

Duncan laughed. "Louie, you kill me. Goats bleat; they don't baa. These are just dogs. We're downwind, or they'd all be barking."

Louie grinned and crunched his shoulder against Duncan's. "This is the place where the lost dogs go."

Duncan shook his head. "Nope. The pound is a brand-new building. These must be hunting dogs, and the owner lives back there in Eastover."

Louie snorted. "I can sure see why he keeps 'em on the back of his lot."

"Any animal stinks if its pen isn't kept clean, Louie. That hunter's a sloppy bum."

Louie stood up, rubbing the bridge rust off his elbows. "Let's beat it before they get wind of us and commence to bark and that sloppy hunter comes barreling out of the woods with a shotgun. First, though, let's take a quick look at this shack. It's all made of doors! Pretty neat."

They crossed the bridge and walked down the path that curved around to the yard in front of the shack. Probably the hunter kept dog food in the shack. One of the doors had a latch with a padlock dangling. But to fiddle with that latch might bring on a chorus from the dogs. Instead they'd settle for a quick look through the two glittering panes of glass. The best position for that would be from the top of the big square abutment that supported this corner of the bridge. It leaned over close to the windows; its slanting surface was big enough to hold two boys lying side by side.

Quickly Duncan and Louie ran back up the path and crawled out on the concrete support. From this perch it was about ten feet down to a prickly-looking patch of weeds watered by the creek. Also on the sandy shore were some old cow bones and a rubber tire.

Through the small window panes part of a bed was visible. It was covered with an army blanket. Louie sat back on his heels. "Somebody lives here, Dunc. Let's scram."

"There's nobody here, Louie. I can see . . . Grab my ankles, Louie. I want to get down a little lower." A copy of *Western Kennel World* lay on the bed. His glance flitted around the room—boxes under the bed, canned goods, a black pot-bellied stove, a calendar. . . .

"Maybe it's an escaped convict, Dunc," Louie whispered anxiously. "Look at those bones down by the water. They could be human bones."

Duncan laughed. "You sound as gruesome as Monroe, Louie. Nobody's here. Hang onto my feet. I can almost—"

"For gosh sakes, don't, Dunc. It might be a lunatic! It isn't any kids' place with a real bed and a stove."

"I know it. It probably belongs to the grubby hunter."

Louie had a tight hold of Duncan's ankles as Duncan hung over the corner of the concrete post, stretched out to his fullest. He felt giddy from the slanting head-heavy position. He must look like a lizard doing push-ups, he thought. "There's a gun in there, Louie. I think it's a gun. It's leaning in a corner. It could be a fishing rod. . . ."

Louie let out a high-pitched yelp and dropped Duncan's feet! Duncan plunged into space. Instinctively he tucked his head under and somersaulted onto his back in the weeds. But the impact of the ten-foot drop knocked the wind out of him. He lay there gasping a few seconds before the din of howling dogs came through to him. He leaped up dizzily, tripped over his own feet, and scraped his arm on the corner of the concrete support he had just fallen from.

Then, panic! Over the brow of the hill, down the curving path plunged the faces and fangs and shaggy chests of five of the strangest- and fiercest-looking dogs he'd ever seen. And behind them towered a gigantic, wildly bearded man, dressed in an old army uniform and yowling and waving one arm. With the other hand he held in check the precipitous charge of the five leashed dogs. The dogs in the pen at the edge of the woods had come awake

too, and they were baying and yapping, leaping and standing on their hind legs against the wire fence.

Duncan stumbled backward into the rubber tire. He leaped up, and running like a deer, sped across the creek. Skimming the surface, he soared as if full of helium, weightless, across the sandy shore to the bank studded with boulders and bird holes, up the slope to the grassy top where Louie's hand reached down and grabbed him, pulled him up till he was on the rutted black road and across it to the bikes.

It seemed to Duncan that his bike was a pigeon weight as he picked it up out of a blackberry bush, spun it around, and shoved off. Once, in the midst of the pell-mell race down the broad dirt path after Louie, he looked back, in a quick glance over his shoulder, a glance that just about wobbled him into the weeds. At the end of the crooked bridge, feet planted wide apart, stood a mountainous man with a white beard down to his waist. And in front of him on leash were five stately dogs, their tongues lolling.

When the country road was a long way behind them, Louie and Duncan stopped pedaling and coasted to a stop at the curb. "I feel like lying down," Louie said in a shaky voice. "Ye gods." He let his bicycle fall and flopped down on the grass in somebody's front yard.

"Me too."

For a long time Duncan and Louie lay panting in the grass without talking. Finally Duncan sat up.

He held his hands out and looked at them. "Lookit, Louie, I'm quivering."

Louie sighed and puffed out his cheeks. "I thought I was going to have a heart attack back there."

"I think I've heard about that old geezer, Louie. He's the hermit with the dogs they talk about."

"Who talks about?"

"Lots of people. Some kids have seen him. You just haven't lived here long enough or you'd have heard about him. He's a recluse."

"Rip Van Winkle, he looked like," Louie said. "And those monster dogs, they'd have massacred us!" Louie rolled over on his stomach in the grass and began to explain what had happened. "I heard this yip, and I looked around and there they were—galloping over that lopsided bridge. I don't know why I dropped you. I just sort of went mushy all over and let go. And they raced past me after you."

"I'm glad you didn't faint. I'm glad you came back and got me up the bank."

Louie pulled at his brown thatch of hair as if trying to straighten out the curls. "Well, after all, I got you into this. Gosh, I'm prickly." He sat up and wiped his sweaty face on his shirttail.

"No, you didn't. It was my idea. I thought it was a shortcut."

"But, it's my paper route. Gimme the money you collected. Did you remember the house with the pillars?"

"It was four in all." Duncan reached into his shirt

25

pocket. It was empty. He rose up on his knees and patted his pants' pockets. Then he sank back on the grass. As he stared at Louie, the whole frantic scene that had just happened rattled through his mind like an episode in an old-fashioned movie. He saw himself topple off the bridge support and sprawl in the weeds by the rubber tire. He imagined the camera moving in to show the four envelopes sliding out of his pocket to disappear under the broad green leaves.

"Oh, my gosh, you lost it!" Louie clapped his hand to his jaw.

Duncan felt in his shirt pocket again. "Oh, no! Thirteen dollars. I added it up. It was right here."

Louie pulled at his hair again and tried to smile. "That's okay. It wasn't your fault."

"What do you mean it wasn't my fault, Louie? Of course it was my fault—my stupid fault. Who's dumb enough to put money in a shirt pocket without a button!" He crossed his legs and jammed his chin down into his hand.

"You sure you put it in your shirt?"

"That's where I put it. Well, don't worry. I'll pay you back."

"I'll split it with you. It was partly my fault."

"No, it wasn't. If you'd had it, it would be in your billfold."

Louie didn't have any answer for that. It was a fact. Louie was careful with money; he had a saving account. It would take a lot of yardwork and car washing to earn thirteen dollars for Louie, but that was the only way to do it. You couldn't go back and ask a crazy old hermit who lived with a pack of vicious dogs if you could look for something you had lost while trespassing on his property.

"I know what," Louie said with a grin, one finger pointing up, a gesture that always announced one of Louie's bright ideas. "He doesn't know we lost anything, so it'll stay where it is—probably in the weeds. All we have to do is to find out when he's gone and then raid the place."

Hmmmmm. "Not a bad idea, Louie."

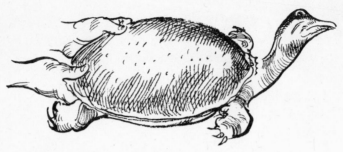

An Introduction to Big Neck

Duncan and Louie burst through the McKennas' back door, arguing. Duncan's mother, who was cooking breakfast, got out of the way. "Mrs. McKenna, your son, Duncan, is a bald-headed liar!" Louie said.

"He is? What's he lying about?"

"That *thing* he caught at Lake Wylie yesterday. Nothing could be *that* weird."

"Louie doesn't believe I've got what I've got in the aquarium, Mom, and don't you tell him."

Louie's forefinger pointed accusingly at Duncan. "He said it's got a head like a horse, a neck like a giraffe, eyes like a frog. . . ."

"No, Louie, I said little black beady eyes like a chameleon and soft like a frog."

". . . and feet like a duck, only frilly. Ye gods! And you said a nose like an anteater and powerful like a bulldog, but without any teeth. Good grief, Duncan. You owe me fifty cents more now; you shook on it. You'd better get going on the yard-work."

"That's fifty cents you're gonna owe *me*," Duncan said.

"And cute—you said cute. Impossible."

Duncan turned on the light over the glass tank that was mounted in a black wrought-iron stand in the McKennas' family room. Water half filled it. Clean white sand covered the bottom.

"It's empty," Louie crowed. "Sorry, old buddy, but it's flown the coop. Where's my fifty cents?"

"You just wait." With a magnifying glass, Duncan peered down at the sand.

"If it's all that infinitesimal sized it doesn't count, Dunc. Naturally there's a lot of microscopic junk that looks weird, but you said 'powerful,' and you didn't say 'powerful for its size.' You said 'like a bulldog.'"

"I said it would hang on like a bulldog."

"But no teeth?"

"Just shut up and sit down, Louie. We've gotta wait." Duncan pulled up two chairs from the break-fast table.

"I bet it's a plain salamander that's buried in there."

"Salamanders are pitiful; they're so weak, Louie. And besides they have hardly any neck."

"Probably some hibernating Siamese fighting fish with black beady eyes. . . ."

"Fish with webbed feet?"

"Well obviously, Duncan, it's got to be a fish." Louie waggled his finger at the aquarium. "It's got to be respiring some way under water with gills."

Duncan sniggered. "Respiring! Where'd you get that word? You must mean breathing."

"No, respiring is what they do with gills. We had it in Science; it's got a respiratory system that can do it under water. That much I know. So it's got to be a fish."

Suddenly at one end of the tank the sand stirred. Duncan grinned a victorious grin at Louie, who rose up out of his chair to stare down at a tiny wormlike protuberance the color of sand and speckled. An inch away from the small tower the sand shivered, and two black dots appeared. "The beady eyes!" Louie said through his fingers. Instantly it disappeared.

"You scared him," Duncan said. "Sit down." Quietly they stared at the sinkhole in the sand made by the disappearing snout. Their breathing misted the glass. Presently it reappeared. The eyes flipped open. The whole slender snout with two nostrils at the end reached up and up and up. A pale long stalk grew out of the sand. It must have seemed to Louie like some quick-growing sea vegetable.

Louie's face went slack. He stood up, holding the

chair in front of him. "Ye gods, a snake. Lemme out of here!"

"You're crazy, Louie. If it were that big a snake, I couldn't leave the top off."

"Wwwwwwwwould that rubbery-looking thing there maybe be only a *neck*?"

"It's a neck. Right. Do you want to see the rest of him?"

"Gulp. Do I want to see the rest of him? Er . . . yeh, sure. Let's have a look at the monster."

Duncan reached into the aquarium with both hands. The long neck retracted. "Watch out. He'll bite you, Dunc. I'm warning you."

"He won't if you know how to grab him." In a storm of flying sand, up came the furious pancake turtle. Frilly webbed feet churned the water and pawed the air. Its head whipped back angrily in an effort to snap the hands that held him, but the enormous neck was unable to stretch out the extra inch that would have let those jaws clamp down on Duncan's wrist.

"Ye gods, ye gods!" Louie lurched backwards, his hands over his face as if he had a toothache on both sides.

Unexpectedly then the turtle calmed down, swiveled its head around to fix on Louie a quizzical frown. Folds of thin shedding skin hung around its legs like lacy pants. The V-shaped chinless lower jaw worked up and down, making a petulant clucking sound like a distressed old man disturbed from a nap before he had time to get his teeth in.

"Ye gods, that's something, that's really something. I've seen it now. Okay, Dunc, you can just ease him back where he came from, if you don't mind."

"It's an Eastern spiny soft-shell, Louie. Fastest kind of turtle there is, on land and in the water too."

"Fine, fine, but ahhhhh, it's dripping on my foot —if you don't mind."

"They call 'em pancake turtles."

Louie nodded and gulped. "Yes, fine. Pancakes with raisins." Duncan backed away a little and Louie blew out a long sigh. "You owe me seven dollars."

"What!"

"In addition to half of that thirteen dollars we lost, you owe me fifty cents."

"You're crazy, Louie. I owe you the whole thirteen, but *you* owe *me* the fifty cents."

Louie shook his head solemnly. "You said 'cute,' and that's the ugliest critter I ever saw."

"He's not ugly. You said yourself he looks like a pancake with raisins. And look, Louie, see those little stripes on his neck, and those worried little black eyes. And feel how soft he is."

"Hey, get away, help!" Louie tripped over Mr. McKenna's wastebasket and slammed into the wall. "Hey, Mrs. McKenna, help! Duncan's going to let this monster bite me." The turtle's long neck lunged

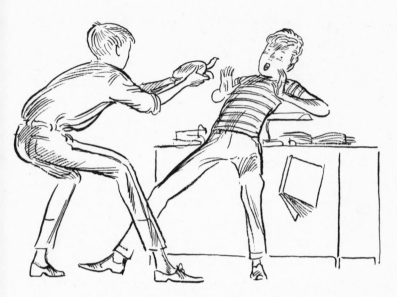

out and his mouth clacked shut, missing Louie's shirt by a thread. "Please, Dunc, I'm not kidding. If he does that again, I'll need a heart transplant. You win. I owe you fifty cents. I'm a liar. The monster's cute, but get him away from me!"

"Duncan, stop pestering Louie," Duncan's mother said, looking into the room. "And please don't drip on the floor."

"Drip on the floor! Mrs. McKenna!" Louie groaned. "And *I* about to be brutally attacked. Duncan, your mother is heartless. She laughed."

Duncan rested his arm on the back of a desk chair. The turtle inspected the things on the desk. Its neck was arched; its chinless mouth chewed slowly as if it were working on a wad of gum. "You have to admit it, Louie. He *is* cute."

"Hmmmm, yes. He's got a kind of cute, aaaaah, proboscis."

"And he's pretty on the bottom, too, Louie." Duncan turned the turtle over. It began to lurch. "Soft as a poached egg."

"Turn him over, turn him over. Ye gods, don't *do* that! He's cuter when he's . . . aaaaah, tranquil."

Back in the aquarium, the turtle stirred up a hurricane of yellow sand and sparkly flakes of mica. It all settled over the broad mottled back when this world's fastest turtle swimmer finally calmed down. Then the aquarium became again a peaceful desert of sand dunes. But under the level of the sand Louie located the turtle's rubbery snout squashed up against the glass. "I see his nose holes. Hey, Big Neck, your nose is bent."

"Big Neck. Hmmmmm. That's a good name for him."

Louie buffed his fingernails on his shirt and blew on them. "Yes, I'm not a bad namer."

"Louie, do you want to have breakfast with us?" Mrs. McKenna called from the kitchen. Louie said he certainly did.

Duncan's father came into the room dressed for church. "How do you like being a paper boy, Louie?" he asked, sitting down at the table.

"It's great. I get twenty-five dollars a week."

"What'll you do with all that money?"

"Oh, lots of things. I'm going to buy me a Cutawl

machine. They cost $350. Jack Pentes, at Pentes Design—he's a friend of mine—said he got a second-hand one at a hockshop when he was thirteen. But I'll have enough money to get a new one."

Duncan wanted to know what a Cutawl machine was. "It's a thing for making cutouts. You gotta have one to be an industrial designer." He turned his attention back to Duncan's father. "And then I'll buy a mechanical-drawing set and a drawing board with a fluorescent light and three sets of Magic Markers and polymer colors and subscriptions to *Display World* and *Art Directions*. I already get *Industrial Design*. And what's left I'll keep for the Rhode Island School of Design."

Duncan's father nodded. "Good, Louie. Sounds like you've got your future mapped."

"I've got 120 papers on my route," Louie continued. "It's a pretty long way because some of the houses are far apart." He put a piece of bacon on his jellied toast and took a big bite. "Mmmmmm, good. Usually I go up one side of the street and down the other so I end up at the pickup where I started, but Dunc and I were all through out there in the country this morning. We tried to come back a different way. . . ." He paused to glance at Duncan. Louie had obviously gotten carried away with his story, and now it looked as if he was either going to make up a lie or blunder into what really took place. That's what happened when kids talked to Duncan's dad. He had the kind of face that without even saying much got people to telling things they hadn't meant to spill. Duncan and Louie had agreed not to tell anyone about what had happened this morning, except their best friends—Gates, Steve, Marshall, and Monroe—who would naturally be in on the plan for getting Louie's money back. Duncan's father wouldn't approve of the idea of their spying on the old man from the woods, so they'd agreed it would be better not to bring it up.

Duncan rushed to Louie's aid, to finish the story without telling an outright lie. "We were starved for a doughnut, so we tried to get over to the doughnut place, but the path wasn't a shortcut, and we came back the same way after all."

"Too bad," Duncan's father said. "You might have discovered some new territory."

"Oh, we did!" Louie exploded. He nodded at Duncan. "I mean about the man on the *sidewalk* with the crazy-looking dogs. It was before daylight even, but here came this huge giant on the sidewalk with these weird-looking dogs, and he had a white beard, and so help me, Mr. McKenna, it came down to here!" Louie stood up, pushing his chair back and held his hand down to his waist. "I'm not kidding."

Mrs. McKenna laughed as she poured a cup of coffee for Duncan's father. "Louie, I think you were dreaming."

Duncan's father shook his head. "No, there *is* such an old fellow here in town. He's a hermit.

Raises Afghan hounds on part of a large tract of land his family used to own somewhere back of the Mint Museum. They say he's a bit balmy."

"See, Louie. He's the old geezer I said he was. I never saw any African dogs before. . . ."

"Afghan hounds," Mr. McKenna corrected. "From the country of Afghanistan. They're one of the oldest breed of dogs in the world. Egyptians used to hunt leopards with them as far back as 4000 B.C. You don't see many Afghans around here."

"I think I saw him once," Mrs. McKenna mused. "He was crossing the street at a green light with a bag of groceries. He had a beard like you said, Louie, and the wind had blown it back over on top of his celery. But he didn't have any dogs with him."

"They've got curly long topknots," Louie said fluffing up his hair, "and their ears are furry too and come down to here under their chins, and they've got wolfish fangs and long curving Roman noses."

"What do you mean he's 'balmy,' Dad? Is he mean?"

"I don't really know, Duncan. I saw him at the park once, but he's a loner—doesn't talk to people except dog-show people. He's a great walker, walks all over town with those dogs. You may get to see him again during the Festival this coming week. I'm told he always puts in an appearance—unscheduled. The Festival Committee tried to get him to come at a certain time to help publicize a dog-training exhibition, but he didn't even answer the letter."

Duncan stabbed a soft-boiled egg with his fork and let the yolk run onto his toast. "How come I've missed seeing him?"

"You're not at the Festival *all* the time, Duncan," his mother said.

"Does he get letters delivered down at his place?" Louie wanted to know.

"Where does he get grocery money?" Mrs. Mc-Kenna asked.

Duncan's father thought he probably had a post office box and a veteran's pension. Not much was known for sure, but in Duncan's mind the hermit became a solid vision, a bearded giant clad in a World War I army uniform with boots, and five fierce dogs to protect him and his property.

"How nuts do you think he is, Mr. McKenna?" Louie asked. "Like, for instance, do you think he'd shoot a person that, aaaaah . . . just wandered into his place by accident?"

Mr. McKenna hesitated, his head cocked at Louie. (And Duncan knew what he was thinking!) "I wouldn't advise anybody to risk it," he said, frowning his bushy light eyebrows together. "If he thought someone was going to try to steal a dog. . . ." He shook his head. "You can never guess what an eccentric will do." Then he grinned confidently. "If you want to see him, just hang around the park this week. You'll probably get a chance to see him make his annual whirlwind tour around the lake."

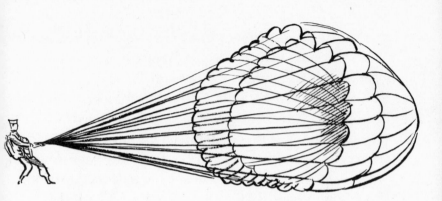

The Parachute Incident

On Monday the story of how Duncan and Louie had almost been killed by a giant and five "African" dogs had swept through the halls and around the playground at Myers Park Elementary School. Steve and Marshall, who were sixth graders like Louie and Duncan, had kept quiet about it. But Monroe and Gates had told a few fifth graders who promised not to tell anybody else. But, of course, they did.

At afternoon recess the six boys met at the parallel bars and discussed the situation. Louie and Duncan could get in plenty of hot water if any of the teachers or Mr. Suber, the principal, heard that they'd been spying in people's windows. So they all agreed to deny everything except that Duncan and Louie on the paper route had seen this old man walking with his dogs. Especially, no one should know of the lost money and the plan to keep watch on the park all week, so that if the hermit came as

Duncan's father thought he would, they could round up the gang and ride to the "shortcut" and a quick search of the weeds by the bridge. If he came when they were in school, they'd be out of luck.

School was finally over, and Duncan sped home on his bicycle with one thing on his mind: Big Neck had to be taken to the turtle pool at the museum. He dropped his book satchel on the dining-room table and went back to the kitchen for a look in the refrigerator. He helped himself to a bunch of grapes, a four-finger pinch of Jello, and from the cookie jar, some stale but decent store-bought cookies.

Gates Lee, his brown eyes narrowed by a big grin, came through the back door, a laundry bag draped around his neck like a towel. "Here's for carrying him in," he said, handing Duncan the laundry bag. He picked off a few of Duncan's grapes. "Thanks." Then he turned on the lamp over the aquarium and peered down at the smooth sand, his hands on his hips, his two front beaver teeth gleaming. "Is he in here, Dunc? Ga! Yeh, I see him. Ha-ha, he thinks I can't see him, but his eyes are just staring at me." Gates's brown silky hair fitted close to his head, adding to his animated Walt Disney beaver look.

Gates had a special interest in Big Neck. It was on a Lee family Saturday picnic at Lake Wylie that Big Neck had been captured. "Let's hurry up and get him over there. He's awful crowded in here. His shell is all bent up on the glass."

"I think I'll put him in my book satchel instead of the laundry bag," Duncan said.

"He'll mess it up like he did the trunk of the car."

"But it'll be easier to carry."

After the usual sport of bringing Big Neck up from his hiding place, the book satchel was loaded and the straps buckled shut. The two boys then set off through Duncan's back yard and the Lees' yard, down the driveway to Sterling Road, sharing the weight of the heaving packsack between them. Duncan paused once to double-check the buckles. They were secure. Big Neck could lurch around all he wanted, but he would never be able to shrug out of the canvas pack.

"Now tell me some more about you and Louie on Sunday morning," Gates said. "Ga, I wish I could have been there!"

"No, you don't, Gates. I was so scared I ran up a practically perpendicular bank. If those dogs had got loose, we'd have been chewed alive."

Gates didn't seem to think this was likely. He grinned and scratched his freckled nose. "And then, like Monroe said, they'd have eaten you up, and there'd be no clues for the police except your bicycles."

"And our belt buckles," Duncan added. "No kidding though, that kind of dog used to hunt antelopes and leopards in ancient times. They *might* have attacked us."

At the corner of Sterling and Princeton, behind

41

the Freedom Park monument, they ducked under some low branches and jogged down through the underbrush into the Lowland Woods. Big Neck, who had calmed down, began humping around again. They came out from under the trees to a view across Sugar Creek of Freedom Park blossoming out for the Festival that was to begin tomorrow. Panel-boards with striped roofs had been set up around the lower end of the lake. Artists were already hanging up their paintings.

Duncan felt sorry for the ducks during the Festival, their territory invaded by foreigners. They were used to lawn mowers, but with the Festival came jeeps, golf carts, trucks, and cars. Overnight, tents sprang up like gaudy mushrooms. And how terrifying to a duck would be the motorboats roaring on the lake, pulling skiers, some of them with kites on their backs that carried them up like weird birds. And then there were the combos on a pontoon boat, loud with electric guitars, drums, and singers. The ducks just took it like bad weather; they huddled together on the island, waiting for it to end.

But the people of Charlotte and the surrounding towns could hardly wait for it to begin. Especially for the children like Duncan and his friends who lived near the park, this was the greatest week of the year. Gates suddenly grabbed Duncan by the arm and shook it. "Jeepers, Dunc, would you look! That's army stuff they're unloading. That's a glider. Let's go see it."

"I can't. I've got to dump Big Neck. You go. I'll see you later." Gates ran off toward the truck on Princeton Avenue, and Duncan continued down the trail on the bank high over Sugar Creek. He was engrossed in the whole buzzing motion of the scene across the creek, his focus constantly shifting as it did at a three ring circus.

The scene was peaceful like the orderly workings of a beehive. Then, without warning . . . *Fooomp,* like dynamite exploding underground up shot the canopy of an orange and white parachute! It was anchored to the ground by many ropes in the hands of an army man who managed them like a Roman charioteer with a team of spirited horses.

Duncan took off like a rocket—raced down the trail, over the footbridge, under a peach tree, and up to the army man. Winded and sweaty, he pulled the heaving book satchel off his back and laid it, right side up, on the grass beside a pup tent and some other army gear.

Duncan had thought parachutes opened only when you jumped out of an airplane and jerked the rip cord. But here was one full as the wind sock at the weather station, billowed up by an ordinary breeze. It couldn't quite make it off the ground for very long at a time, but it skipped and bounced on its side rolling counterclockwise as the army man sidestepped along the grass, the cords twisting till the army man said, "Whoa," and made it return. The wind slackened a little; the parachute flopped and threatened to drop in a heap of limp silk; the soldier stepped backward, tensing the cords. There was a hollow smack and the white and orange sail took a quick deep breath. . . .

Duncan felt as he had when for the first time he looked down into the Grand Canyon and saw its stripes of different-colored rock, signifying millions of years. Only this parachute was a modern achievement. How he would love to take hold of those ropes!

The young army man smiled down at Duncan. "I expect you'd like to try it. Sorry, but it's against regulations." He wore a patch on his sleeve—Eighty-second Airborne Division, United States Army.

People gave the parachute a lot of room. Even the black and white dog that belonged to Mr. Garringer, the park superintendent, passed at a safe distance and gave out a few suspicious woofs. But from behind, something attacked the ballooning silk. Something like a head butted into it; then many smaller dents peppered it.

"Some jackass back there smarting off," the army man remarked.

People began to gather around, smiling. Among the spectators to this sideshow was an eighth-grade jerk named Conway Sides, a friend of Duncan's worst enemy, Van Meyerding. Conway was flapping his bony elbows and giving out a feeble whinny. Duncan felt his blood pressure rise. The smart jackass was surely Van Meyerding.

Van probably wouldn't have been so bad if Duncan had been able to stay out of his way. But the park was their common neighborhood. The choice came often—to meet Van's smirk head-on with a smirk of his own, or to turn around and beat it. Duncan could never get himself to run like a scared rabbit from Van. Consequently he had often been the butt of Van's judo demonstrations. Van kept a paperback judo book in his back pocket the way a little kid wears cowboy guns.

"It's *him*," Duncan muttered, feeling the old familiar bristling along his spine.

"Let's get him," the paratrooper said, giving Duncan a wink. "Watch me louse up this guy."

He backed up quickly, giving the ropes a jerk that caused the parachute to hop off the grass, higher than it ever had before. There stood Van in tight white jeans and a yellow sweat shirt that said THE INCREDIBLE HULK across its front. His hand was poised for a chop.

"I got him," the soldier chuckled. He ran forward and let up on the ropes. The parachute dropped, and the loose ropes fell around Van, snaring him till he was enmeshed like a bug in a spider web. Then the soldier tugged the reins, and the wind filled out the silk again.

Van's fancy judo form was gone as he struggled frantically to escape from the ropes. No sooner would he slip out of one snare than several others would wind around him as the chute rolled over the grass, dragging Van along with it. Finally Van yelled out hoarsely, "Hey, watch it, bud," and fell to his knees, his feet in a tangle.

As if seeing Van's plight for the first time, the army man said, "Would you look! I've caught me a civilian. Do pardon me, sir."

Duncan was convulsed with laughter. He reeled around. Ha, ha, ha—oh, gosh, the Hulk on his knees! Hee, hee, hee—a praying mantis caught in a web! What a blast he'd have telling his friends; he'd act it out, he'd have them dying of laughter. His stomach was sore from laughing, but he couldn't stop—even though he felt Van's burning eyes upon him.

Where was the book satchel? A tide of sanity dumped down on him as he looked at the vacant space beside the pup tent.

"Where's the jeep and all that stuff?" he asked the army man.

"Up the hill, I guess."

"Whereabouts 'up the hill'? I've got to find it."

"Could be back at the van or up at the aid station. We're just getting organized around here. Some of that was first-aid stuff brought over here by mistake."

"My book satchel's gone. They must have picked it up!"

The man laughed. "Now you've got a perfect excuse not to do your homework."

"But it doesn't have books in it. It's got my turtle."

46

"Your what?"

"My turtle. It's a big soft-shell. I was taking him to the museum. I can't lose him. I've got to find him!" Duncan's voice rose shrill.

"All right, now, just a minute." The parachute fluttered to the ground.

"It was right here by a bedroll, and now it's gone. Where's the jeep? Somebody must have put it in the jeep. Where's the jeep? They might have just thrown it in, and it's squashed under a Coleman stove and the bedroll and all. . . ."

"Simmer down now, son. We'll find it. It's probably at the first-aid station. That's where it's at. We'll go check soon as I gather up this chute." Duncan was dimly aware of Van behind him, whispering to Conway Sides. "Hold on till I get the key to the storage room. They might have locked it up already." Duncan waited impatiently as Conway and Van ran off along the lake shore and the man picked up the parachute and tossed it under the tent flap. "Hey, wake up, Buzz," he called into the tent. "I gotta leave awhile. Gimme that storage key."

When Duncan and the soldier rounded the corner of the lake, they could see at the top of the hill the jeep parked by the first-aid station. Duncan heaved a relieved sigh. "I just hope he isn't suffocated under a bedroll or something."

"Turtles are tough," the army man said. "There's the fellow we caught in the ropes. I should apologize to him, I guess. He looked mighty hot and bothered."

47

"Don't bother. It's me he's mad at. He hates me."

"Why? Did you steal his girl?"

"Ha. Funny. He doesn't like girls. He thinks he's a judo hotshot. Nobody his age likes him, so he has to pester us kids."

All of a sudden, with a click in his head, Duncan realized what he was seeing—*his* book satchel over Van's shoulder! "Look! He's got my turtle. He heard me tell you. I might have known he'd do something like that to pay me back."

Duncan ran in front of a slow-moving truck, leaving behind the paratrooper who waited for it to pass. He intercepted Van and Conway at the sidewalk that banded the hill like a belt halfway up. Van, his face in a smirk, relaxed into a slouch, his thumb tucked under the strap that went over his right shoulder.

"That's my book satchel," Duncan said, reaching for it.

Van sidestepped him and continued to saunter on down the hill. "What's it worth to you?"

"Give it to me. It's mine. There's nothing in it you'd want."

"I know, a turtle. I know a guy'll give me a dollar for one this size. For a dollar you can have it."

"I don't have to pay for what's already mine!" Duncan made a grab for the book satchel, but Van was ready. He hooked his heel around Duncan's ankle, gave him a push with the flat of his hand.

Duncan sprawled backward, his hands sinking into the black mud at the edge of the lake.

Furiously he struggled up, flipped the mud off his hands, and reveled in images of what he'd like to do to Van Meyerding—trip him, sprawl him, smear him with mud, and laugh. "Ha, ha, ha," he sneered at Van, his fury spinning. "You're so darn smart . . . you're a big . . ." He edged up, dancing like a boxer, hoping for a chance to swoop in and snatch the book satchel from behind. "You're a big s . . . s . . . s. . . ." He had been all set to say "stupid jerk" when he saw something that got him to stuttering.

The flap of the book satchel had slowly folded back beside the buckle, and out emerged a few inches of Big Neck. Desperately Duncan tried to hang onto his mad look so as not to warn Van. He forced a fiercer frown, smothered down what he wanted to do—to burst out in wild glee. Poor Van! Just under his ear the little black eyes blinked and the chinless mouth hung open like the grin of a mischievous old man. Poor Van—his ear!

Here came the soldier now, his eyes on the head of Big Neck, his mouth open in astonishment. Conway, on the other side of Van, couldn't see the odd sight. And now up ran Monroe, Duncan's baby-faced friend. He pointed at Van and squealed, "Hey, what you got there, Van?"

But Van didn't get the warning. He probably thought he was being teased for carrying a book satchel—Junior Highs never did. He snorted and casually reached up with his hand, probably to jerk the knapsack off his shoulder. And then it happened. With wide open jaws and the thrust of his whole neck, Big Neck lunged, catching Van across the knuckle of his first finger.

"*Aaaawwwwwkkkk!*" Van let out a hoarse scream and tore his hand away. Blood streamed down his fingers and dripped on his white pants and his tennis shoes. He stared for a moment, transfixed, at his trembling, bleeding hand. Then with his left hand he swung the book satchel in a loop twice around his head and let go. It sailed out over the crape-myrtle bushes, high over the lake, and then down like a rock just off the shore of the island.

Duncan was running when it lit and sank, leaving a few bubbles and ripples on the placid water. Behind him he could hear Van's strenuous cursing and the paratrooper's reassurances that the hand could be dressed at the first-aid station.

Duncan ran across the wooden bridge to the island. Often this island was a stage for plays and concerts. The audience would sit on the green benches on the mainland, watching the performance across a narrow channel of water.

He headed in what seemed the right direction, but when he emerged from behind a row of junipers, panting and peeling off his shirt, there before him was the sparkling crystal fountain. Duncan liked that fountain but not now. It meant he was way off

course. The splashdown must have been farther to the left. He wasn't sure where Big Neck fell, only that it was near the shore and not near the fountain.

Duncan dropped his shoes and shirt and ran out into the water to begin the search. Big Neck would be okay; a turtle can stay under water a long time. Rotting leaves on the lake bottom gave the water a clear iced-tea color, but now with Duncan stirring up the mud, it become too murky to see through.

Monroe came splashing out to join Duncan. "He's got to have a tetanus shot. Van's gonna have a shot," he crowed.

"I hope it hurts," Duncan mumbled. "You look along the shore, Monroe. I'll cover it out here."

Monroe saluted. "Right, chief."

Back and forth systematically Duncan plowed, feeling with his bare feet every inch of the lake bottom up to the edge of the fountain spray. Water clung to his jeans, and the mud sucked his feet down. He stiffened his mind against worrying, but as the minutes passed and the water felt more and more like molasses, a heavy anxiety weighed him down. He ached all over. His arms and legs, his lungs and heart—he was too tired to move, but he kept on. Where *was* that book satchel? No, not the book satchel. Who cared about a book satchel? You could get another secondhand for a quarter. But Big Neck. . . .

Monroe called to him that it was time to quit, that in his opinion Big Neck had worked his feet out of the satchel and was going after the fish in the middle of the lake, where it was deep.

Duncan felt like crying. He knew Big Neck couldn't escape, but he couldn't search any longer. He was too tired to move another step. Suddenly though an eerie sensation gripped him. *Something* had him by the foot!

He felt jaws cutting into his ankle. Savagely he tried to jerk his foot loose, but the *thing*—whatever it was—clung tight around his ankle. Over and over the sensible part of his mind affirmed, there's no thing in this lake with a mouth big enough to grab a whole foot! But his heart hammered wildly, and with new strength surging through him, he tore at the *thing* with his hands, forcing "it" to let go.

The feel was familiar. Yes. In his trembling hands was an old hard-rubber volleyball with a jagged split like a grinning mouth. Duncan had to laugh—a tired giggle—at this gruesome, ill-timed joke. He dropped the volleyball, and when he could breathe normally again, he lay floating face down in the water. When the mud settled, maybe he could see the bottom, maybe a glint of light would catch on a brass buckle or the long tan snout of Big Neck. By now though, it seemed hours had passed. It could be too late. It would be better not to find Big Neck at all than to find him dead.

But Duncan wasn't to float there long, his stinging eyes straining to see through the tea-colored lake. He was "attacked" again. Strong arms lifted him up out of the water like huge grappling eels, and as if a live wire had touched him, Duncan lashed out with fists and feet.

This time his struggle was over almost instantly. He heard a familiar voice. "For Lord's sake, Duncan, you like to scared me to death!" It was poor Mr. Garringer puffing and holding his big stomach where Duncan had kicked him. His green park superintendent's jacket was a wet dark green up to the pockets. He sighed and passed his broad freckled hand over his nearly bald head.

Duncan couldn't even mumble for several minutes. He just stood there panting, with the mud squishing between his toes, his bleary eyes fixed on Mr. Garringer's wet clothes. "I'm sorry, Mr. Garringer," he finally said. "Why'd you come out here? Did you think I was somebody drowned?"

"Confound it, Duncan. What else was I to think, somebody lyin' still in the water, not movin' at all? Why'd you have to get in the lake, Duncan, you and Monroe here? You know the park rules."

"I'm sorry, Mr. Garringer. We didn't do it for fun. My turtle's out there someplace, and he's probably drowned by now."

"Good heavens, boy. You can't drown a turtle."

Monroe, who had been nervously twisting the wet bottom of his UNC sweat shirt, nodded vigorously at that. "That's what I say too, Mr. Garringer. Ha-ha, you can't drown a turtle. Right?"

"But this one was in my book satchel," Duncan

said. He explained it to Mr. Garringer as they walked slowly across the island stage and over the bridge to the mainland. Mr. Garringer's shoes squished with every step.

"Hey, Mr. Garringer, sir." Monroe giggled, his dimples in deep. "Ha-ha, you sure got some noisy shoes there."

Mr. Garringer nodded. "Started out, I was looking for you boys anyway," he said. "Didn't think I'd have to go fishin' for you."

"What did you want us about?" Duncan asked.

"Just to be sure you know about Saturday. My friend Gumpi Kawada is bringing his judo classes out here to put on a show. You don't want to miss it. I told your friend, Gates Lee, just now. He's over where they're setting up an army exhibit. You all pass the word around. Want a good crowd out."

Duncan and Monroe had often heard Mr. Garringer brag about this friend of his who taught judo at the Y. This Gumpi had apparently sold Mr. Garringer on the idea that everybody ought to take judo, especially Van Meyerding. But Duncan could hardly go along with that. Van was a menace with his self-taught variety of judo. How much worse he'd be after some expert teaching! Mr. Garringer didn't stay long to talk this time. He had to go and change his clothes.

"Who wants to watch ol' Van Meyerding show off his judo?" Monroe said, screwing up his small dimpled face. "Not me! I hate his guts. Too bad what he did to your turtle." But Monroe didn't spend any time being sorry for the turtle. "I wonder how it would feel to suffocate to death," he said with a grin.

Then he grabbed himself around the neck and squeezed till his face turned shockingly pink, his blue eyes bulged, and he staggered around making gurgling noises in his throat. A group of little girls stopped to stare at him, and then giggled when it was all over and Monroe turned pale again.

Duncan shoved him into a crape-myrtle bush. "You're gruesome, Monroe."

Monroe was also the most reckless of Duncan's friends. It was Monroe who had favored immediate action to get back Louie's money. During the big planning session Sunday afternoon on how to proceed to the hermit's shack, Monroe had insisted that the best way to do it would be to get up at three A.M. and go out there with flashlights to search those bushes while the hermit was asleep.

"He'll be in there snoring his head off," Monroe had said with great confidence. "Sure, Monroe," Louie had answered, "and then he'll wake up and come out with his gun and shoot *our* heads off."

"Hey, I wonder if Van's got his stitches in yet," Monroe said. "They wouldn't let me watch."

He ran off, and Duncan was glad. He wasn't in the mood for Monroe's grisly sense of humor.

The Cheetah

Duncan ran across the grass and over the foot-bridge to the cheetah cage behind the Nature Museum. The cheetah ambled over to the fence. She was always glad to see him, though her face never smiled and her yellow eyes never looked at him directly. She would gaze at far-off scenes as if scanning the distance for antelope.

On the wire of her cage, under her scientific name, *Acinonyx jubatus,* was a short description of the cheetah, "the fastest mammal on earth." And beside this was a poem, framed and under glass:

THE CHEETAH AND THE FOUNTAIN
by Paul Baker Newman

The cheetah
and his eyes like big
glass lanterns in his head
lolls in the hot April with
high winds and the fresh

57

sweet grass spring-
ing up in bunch-
es near his cage,
the air pouring through the high
leaves so fresh and scarcely ripened
and the dogwood making clouds
of just-opened not quite white
like the rind of a green melon
the ground gravelly and washed
level with the tree-
roots terraced
in the red mud of the paths.
Beside the fountain
a black-
bird dogfights with a crow,
and the cheetah watches with yellow eyes wide open and unflick-
ering like two head-
lamps in the silence
that he makes in all that motion.

Duncan read that poem every time he stopped at
the cheetah cage. It always brought on a prickly
feeling along his arms and made him look again into
the cheetah's big yellow eyes and then across the
lake at the fountain.

The cheetah flopped down by the corner post
where Duncan was putting on his shoes. She purred
a deep rumble in her throat and offered her small
round ear for Duncan to scratch. He ruffled the fur
of her ear and all around it as far as he could reach
through the chain-link fence.

Suddenly the cheetah's purr cut off, and her head

flew up; she bounded to the center of her large enclosure. Down the trail rattled three boys on bicycles.

"It's okay, girl. It's okay, cheetah girl. Come on back, they're gone now. They're not going to bother you. . . ." The boys were gone, but still her lantern-yellow eyes stayed fixed on the path where it entered the woods. The end of her long spotted tail continued to twitch.

Chicken wire roofed over the cheetah pen. It was sagged down with sticks and rocks that had been lobbed up there by the kind of boys the cheetah feared—boys on bicycles who scraped the wire with sticks and sometimes even threw lighted cherry bombs at her.

The purr was beginning again, like a motor inside idling. She lay on the ground close to the fence and moved her head languidly against Duncan's fingers. A mother with three small boys in baseball caps came up and asked him some questions about the cheetah. The cheetah had once been the mascot of the Charlotte Motor Speedway, he told her, but not any more. She was too old and lazy to run fast. Seven was getting old for a cheetah. Her owner, Bob Casey, paid her food bill to the Nature Museum— six hundred dollars' worth of horsemeat a year.

When finally Duncan stood up to go, the cheetah lifted her spotted head and gave him a serious brief glance. Then her eyes shifted across the creek to the park, now dressed for the Festival, and the fountain, a white sparkling umbrella in the sun.

The back door to the museum was locked, of course. It was long after five. It felt like almost six. Duncan's father was coming out the front door when Duncan rounded the corner. "Hi, Dad, did you come in the car today?" Mr. McKenna walked to work when he didn't have a meeting to go to.

"Yes, I had 'The Joey Show.' Took the baby armadillo." Duncan's father or somebody from the museum was always on Joey the Clown's Monday TV show.

"I wish I'd stayed home and watched it. If I'd stayed home, I'd still have Big Neck. Blast it all, Dad, I hate Van Meyerding. You know what he did?" Duncan jerked open the car door, and bristling mad again, slammed it behind him. As his father drove toward home, he spun out the details of his run-in with Van Meyerding, how he had laughed when Van got tangled up in the parachute ropes, how Big Neck had bitten Van, and then Van's terrible revenge.

"Are you sure you looked in the right place, Duncan? Maybe it fell in shallow water. It's only a couple feet deep around the fountain. With his head free, even if he landed upside down. . . ."

His dad was trying to make him feel better. But it didn't help. It made it worse, in fact, because he now learned that a soft-shell can live up to two hours under water. His larynx has a special lining that can take oxygen out of the water like a gill. Big Neck had been *alive* when he gave up the search. He could have got other kids to help. Mr.

Garringer would have let them use his leaf rakes; they could have got an underwater flashlight. He mourned all over again until his father said sternly, "Duncan, stop all this misery. You did what you could."

"I hate Van Meyerding."

"How do you suppose Van felt? Suddenly right under his ear a hideous creature appears and bites his hand down to the bone. If you were Van, just how would that grab *you*? You might heave it in the lake too."

"Big Neck isn't hideous."

The car swung around the corner to Maryland Avenue. Mr. McKenna gave Duncan a swat on the knee. "Uh, huh, I know. He's cute."

"It's not funny, Dad. Why do you have to defend Van? There's nothing good about him. He's mean. Even Mr. Garringer admits it. He's trying to think up ways to improve him. He's got a crazy idea that taking judo lessons at the Y would help. But Van already knows enough about how to trip you and flip you and strangle you with a sleeper around the jugular till you pass out cold."

"Duncan, you exaggerate."

"He's tried it, and he's flipped lots of us, especially me."

"See that you stay out of his way, Duncan. It probably bugs him for you to go around like you do with snakes around your neck and man-eating turtles in your rucksack. No doubt he was scared to death of your friend, Big Neck. And with you being so much smaller than he is, that's enough to rile him."

Now *there* was a satisfying idea. Maybe a few times in his life Duncan had actually scared Van Meyerding.

"By the way, Duncan, Joey's going to do some filming at the fairgrounds to promote the fair. He'll need our biggest snake and the cheetah. Would you like to be the snake handler? It'll be Wednesday afternoon. I could write a note to Mr. Suber and get you out early."

Oh, boy! There was another satisfying idea! He bounded out of the car and up the kitchen steps. "Hey, Mom, I'm going to be on TV!" He swung open the refrigerator door. But what if the hermit came on Wednesday afternoon? . . . Oh, no.

"Now, wait a minute," his father said. "I didn't say that. They just need somebody to handle the snake between shots. That's where you come in."

Duncan's mother put a tray of biscuits in the oven. "What's all this about? Stay out of the refrigerator, Duncan."

Duncan must have come out of the refrigerator with a long face. His father said, "If you don't want to do it, just say so. We'll get somebody else."

"No, I want to do it."

"Well, *what* then?"

"I . . . I. It's just that I remember what you said, uh, about that old hermit coming to the park. We—

Louie and I and the rest of us—we just want to get a look at him and those dogs, is all. Do you really think he'll come, Dad?"

"He'll come, all right, but you never know when. Daytime though—he's not likely to come at night."

It would be the worst kind of bad luck if the hermit appeared at just the one time Duncan wasn't around. He could hardly bypass this chance to meet Joey the Clown in person and watch him make a movie with a snake and the cheetah. But if the hermit should come on Wednesday, the raid would naturally have to go on without him. It hardly seemed fair though since he was the one who had lost the money.

The idea of receiving a signal, racing to a target area, searching for lost treasure while vicious dogs bayed and a lunatic old man might burst in on them at any moment—this would be exhilarating business. It would, he knew, also be—as his father would put it—dangerous, illegal, and devious, not the way to go about solving a problem. However—

Duncan's mother laughed. "He just doesn't want to miss a single minute of the Festival, David. What's all this about Joey?"

"Just a publicity stunt for the Mecklenburg County Fair, Jane. Bob Casey will bring his cheetah, and Duncan will take charge of the pine snake."

"What does the snake have to do?" Duncan asked.

"Scare Joey. Joey'll get into one scrape after another. The cheetah will chase him too. You'll just let the snake loose, when they tell you to, and then catch it again. It'll crawl under a fence or something and scare Joey out of his wits."

Duncan's mother shook her head as she turned over some pork chops that were cooking on the stove. "Aw, Mother, the snake won't hurt him." His mother knew that; what she didn't like was the idea of letting the cheetah out of her cage. "She's a wild animal, and you shouldn't forget it," she said.

"But she's tame, Mother. She loves Mr. Casey and me too. She's used to people. After all, she was the mascot of the Motor Speedway."

"I know, and I think it's cruel to make her run beside a car going sixty miles an hour."

"Nobody makes her. She does it for fun," Mr. McKenna said. "Or used to. They don't run her anymore."

"I still say wild animals are unpredictable. They should either be left in the wild or kept in cages."

"This one never was wild. She was raised on a bottle by a safari hunter's wife."

"Wash your hands and come to supper, Duncan."

"They're clean."

"Honestly, Duncan, I'm sure you haven't washed them since you handled that big turtle after school."

Duncan groaned. "Why'd you have to bring that up?" Poor Big Neck. He turned the light off over the empty aquarium. "He's dead, Mom. Best turtle I ever had. He was going to be a science project, and it's all that blasted Van Meyerding's fault. If

I just knew some judo tricks Van doesn't know, he'd come along, and I'd slip in and flip him so fast—"

"Duncan, we're not going into *that* again," his father said. "Wash your hands and come to the table."

One thing Duncan's father didn't allow was dragging things out. And actually Duncan was glad to let it drop. Thoughts of Van Meyerding would ruin his appetite. The supper smelled good, and Duncan was suddenly caved in with starvation. He washed his hands at the kitchen sink, flipped them in the air a few times, and sat down.

After a bite of pork chop scooped into the mashed potatoes, he felt much better. "Well, anyway, I still want to build a pool in the backyard and have a waterfall connected to the hose. In the spring we can have a mammoth collecting trip to Lake Wylie and catch a lot of baby necks."

"Baby whats?" his mother asked.

"Soft-shells, Mom. Is that all right, Dad—to build a pool? We can use the sand from the sandbox; I don't need it anymore."

It was all right with Duncan's father. A pool could be useful for hatching out tadpoles and breeding other pond life for the limnology classes at the museum. His mother thought it would be lovely for water lilies. It would be handy for filling squirt guns during squirt-gun fights, Duncan thought, but mainly it would be for turtles—a memorial to Big Neck.

The Festival Begins

Duncan heard Gates yelling bloody murder in the backyard. He put his books on the dining-room table and ran to the window. Tony, Duncan's raccoon, was back! He'd been gone for several days. Now, draped like a coonskin cap over Gates's head, he was busily patting every bare inch of skin on Gates's face. Gates's book satchel fell to the ground as Tony slid down headfirst into his arms.

"Hi, Tony, where've you been?" Duncan said as he ran up. But Tony had found in Gates's pants pocket some crinkly paper left from a package of peanut-butter crackers; he was too busy rustling the paper even to pause at the familiar sound of Duncan's voice.

"This raccoon's gone nuts, Dunc. Get him." Gates's face was all puckered up in an effort to escape Tony's tickly ringed tail.

"He's probably hungry. Come here, Tony." Now,

like a baby, Tony leaned into Duncan's arms. "You crazy coon, calm down." A raccoon's paw, unlike a monkey's, can't pick things up and hold on, but the two together can knead almost anything out of shape. Duncan's nose was being mashed, patted, and pressed flat like dough in the hands of a baker. Then with his sharp teeth Tony nipped the end of it. Duncan tossed him out on the grass. "You biter!" he scolded, rubbing his almost punctured nose. Tony humped around in a circle, raced back to playfully attack Duncan's leg. With all four clawed feet he hung on as Duncan braced himself on an apple-tree bough and shook his leg vigorously. Tony clung tightly, growling, his teeth sunk in the blue-jean material. His pudgy body swayed like a jungle hammock.

"He's sure glad to be back," Gates said. "Where do you think he's been?"

"Messing around in Sugar Creek probably. He wouldn't find many crayfish there anymore though. The city's crowding it too much." Tony was content to be quiet in Duncan's arms now, chewing and patting the collar of his shirt. "Sometime when he goes exploring he might not come back."

"A dog could get him," Gates said.

"We ought to take him out to Lake Wylie pretty soon and let him go. He'll want to find a place to hibernate for the winter."

It would be lonesome without Tony around, but after all, he wasn't a dog who would be your friend for life. You could hardly want to hang onto a pet who'd wake up from hibernation ready to bite you. "I wish I'd left Big Neck out there to hibernate," Duncan said, shredding a leaf with his thumbnail.

Gates, always sympathetic about Duncan's problems, looked at him with round, earnest brown eyes and suggested that maybe somehow Big Neck had escaped from the book satchel and was alive and happy in the Freedom Park lake. "Anyway," he added, "if he died, it was a heroic way to die, after biting Stupid Meyerding to the bone."

Duncan agreed with that. He got some fish heads out of the freezer for Tony, and he and Gates left him growling happily over them, dipping them in and out of his water dish.

Today at the park would be the wrong day for the hermit to come for his annual whirlwind tour. The place was swarming! He and his dogs would be bogged down to the slow pace of an ordinary Festival browser.

At the Sedgefield School exhibit, soberly working away at an artist's easel, was baby-faced, wild-man Monroe. Gates nudged Duncan as they came up to the rope. Look at who's in the kindergarten."

"Have you been keeping a lookout for the hermit, Monroe?" Duncan asked.

Monroe wiped his hands on his long UNC sweat shirt and laughed. "Hah! No sign of Santa Claus and his five African reindeer, ha-ha. Truth is, fellas, they

won't get here till December twenty-fifth." Monroe sailed off into shrill giggles.

"What a moron," Gates said to Duncan.

Farther up the lake shore—past the art work, the Carolina Clowns and the Goodwill Industries—was the exhibit of the Eighty-second Airborne Division.

"That's the man who goofed up Van Meyerding," Duncan told Gates and Monroe.

The paratrooper was laying his parachute out in a circle and making a speech. "This is a thirty-foot canopy across the diameter. That's regulation for all predetermined jumps." He caught sight of Duncan and gave him a salute. "Come on up front, boys. This bright color here is not just for looks, folks. It can be spotted a long way off and is an aid in the pickup of a downed pilot. In actual war conditions over enemy territory, fighter pilots will use camouflaged chutes so they won't be seen by the enemy. They're packed with two packets of chaff. That's a metal foil which disperses out in the air when the chute is opened. Then radar picks it up on the screen. We get a location fix on the chaff and are able to rescue the pilot."

As he listened, Duncan scanned the shoreline for the tall bearded man with his Afghan dogs.

The paratrooper finished spreading out the parachute and the ropes neatly on the ground. "There's thirty cords attached to the skirt at regular intervals." Deftly he put pleats in the thirty panels till it was all gathered into a tall triangle, the peak being the center of the canopy. The suspension cords he laid out in parallel lines. "Now we're ready to fold the gores."

Monroe giggled. "Gory business, ha-ha." Gates and Duncan elbowed him in the ribs.

"The little fella's got a point there, folks." The man smiled at Monroe. "You can't be too careful about packing a chute, or it *will* be gory business. Before it's folded, the canopy must be inspected for damaged and weak spots, mildew, rust, oil stains, and battery acid, which deteriorate the fabric rapidly." It sounded as if he had memorized the book.

Now he had the loose folds in two separate stacks. He threw one stack over on top of the other. "That leaves one more gore, this here between lines fifteen and sixteen." He pounded a tent peg into the ground to hold the lines in place during the next operation, the careful folding. He explained all this as he meticulously pulled the panels tight and neat like the bottom sheet of a bed. "Hey, Buzz, throw me the shot bags." Buzz, the other paratrooper, ducked under the pup-tent flap and came out with what looked like three long beanbags which he threw one by one to his friend. They clinked when they were caught as if full of bb's. They were laid along the straight edge of the group of fifteen tightly folded panels. Then the other fifteen rough folds were made tight and straight.

"Now," he said, "you stow the suspension lines

like so and then the canopy. Do it opposite, and you get yourself hung in the ropes. Right?" He pointed at Monroe. Monroe nodded vigorously. When the chaff was stowed and the canopy accordion folded and laid on top of the lines and the pack closed securely, the paratrooper stood up, a satisfied look on his face.

When the exhibition was over, the crowd began to drift away. "You sure do know a lot about parachutes, sir," Monroe said, shaking his head, his face beetled up in a frown.

"That's why they've got me over here," the soldier said, sitting down on the grass with the boys. "You can call me Fred. That's my name."

An idea popped into Duncan's mind then. "Hey, Fred, I just thought of something." Fred could be a lookout! "Are you going to be over here all week?"

"Yup. Buzz and I take turns with the demonstration."

Duncan asked him then if he'd keep his eyes peeled for a huge, bearded old hermit in a World War I uniform and some big dogs on a leash. Fred said he'd be sure to notice a fellow who looked like that. "I'll try to hold him awhile. You just check back from time to time."

"You can't hold him," Duncan said. "My dad says he only talks to people with show dogs. Or else if you want to buy a puppy."

"What's your phone number? I'll tell him some boys want to buy a puppy."

Simultaneously Gates, Monroe, and Duncan protested. "No, don't tell him that!"

Fred laughed and scratched his stubbly army haircut. "I thought you wanted to see him about something."

"Not *about* anything, just *see* him," Gates said, chewing his thumbnail.

"We don't really need to see him either," Monroe said with a weak grin. Duncan stepped meaningfully on Monroe's foot, and Monroe added quickly, "But we'd like to. From a distance." He twisted the bottom hem of his light-blue sweat shirt into a long spiral and beamed at the soldier.

The conversation was so messed up that Duncan felt he ought to say something sensible. "They're Afghan dogs, and Afghan puppies are very expensive," he said. "Also he's sort of odd-looking. I saw him once. My dad says he always comes to the Festival sometime during the week."

Fred gave Duncan a rough pat on the back. "I think you guys are scared of this old bird. He fascinates you like a snake."

"And you ought to see his fearsome-looking dogs," Monroe said, scowling and making claws of his hands. He backed up, tripping over a tent peg, caught at the guy rope, and almost brought the pup tent down, which abruptly ended the conversation.

"What a moron," Duncan and Gates said to the paratrooper.

The swingingest place at the Festival that first

afternoon was the amateur folk singers' tent. The microphone was turned up loud, and a crowd of volunteers hung around waiting to be urged. "Michael, Row the Boat Ashore" was now being belted out.

"If I didn't know better, I'd swear that was Steve," Duncan said. Steve had been working on that song since August when he bought a guitar with his grass-cutting money. But Steve couldn't sound that good, though Duncan often said, and he meant it, that Steve could do about anything he tried to do. He got straight A's. He read *Popular Science* from cover to cover and knew a lot more about science than Miss Frazer, their sixth-grade science teacher. *She* even admitted it. But one thing Duncan knew—Steve's voice was feeble.

"It *is* Steve!" Gates said, jumping up for a view over the heads of people.

"It can't be!" Duncan insisted.

They pushed into the crowd and saw that it certainly *was* Steve. The sun glistened on his owlish round glasses and on his big skin-diver's watch. His heel pounded the grass and his blond hair bounced.

What made Duncan look around he didn't know, but he did, and his glance caught on Paula. What a jolt! Skinny, bouncy, green-eyed, sun-tanned Paula! That girl made a blithering idiot out of Duncan, transformed him at a glance into a clumsy, tongue-tied oaf. Furious with his stupidly galloping heart, he sneaked another look, careful that Monroe

75

and Gates, who hated girls, didn't see him do it. She watched Steve with a glistening smile and twiddled a pearl that hung on a gold chain around her neck. A hot guilty wave of jealousy rolled over Duncan. He wished the microphone would drop dead! Brusquely he whispered to Gates, "Let's go." Monroe had moved up front and was sitting on the grass.

"Steve's going to get conceited," Duncan grumbled when he and Gates were away from the thundering volume of the microphone.

"Do you think he's that good?"

"No, but some people seem to think so. Let's go see THE HAPPENING."

Another big crowd surrounded THE HAPPENING, a something-or-other that from a distance looked as if it had beeped in from another planet. But before Duncan and Gates were close enough to get a good look, four boys whom Duncan had never seen before came to a halt in front of them.

One of them had a red balloon with "Park Band Shell" spelled out on it in white letters. In a weird high voice he squeaked, "Take me to your leader!" In the same thin voice the others squealed at Duncan and Gates, "Quick, or we'll melt you!" Then all four began a shrill cackle so strange that it sent shivers up Duncan's backbone.

Gates was as shaken as Duncan. He stared back at Duncan with his brown eyes open so wide that the whites were a ring around them. From such

77

ordinary-looking boys had come such freakish sounds! And now they were gone—vanished.

"What in the heck was that?" Duncan whispered.

"Martians, ha-ha. There they are, Dunc, at the architect's tent. Let's trail 'em."

In a corner by some photographs of buildings the four "Martians" huddled. They seemed to be blowing up the balloon. No, the balloon was getting smaller. Each one took a turn. "Gates, they're breathing that helium!"

The huddle broke up, and the four with fierce grins on their faces planted themselves in front of two teen-age girls who had been looking at the model of a new shopping mall. The cackling of four Donald Ducks swelled up to the tent roof. Everyone looked up in astonishment. But all they saw was four boys running out under the Exit sign.

"I know what. It's the helium that queers up their voices, Dunc. I saw it in a comic once. These deep-sea divers came up from exploring a sunken ship, and everybody laughed at everybody else."

Duncan nodded. "It keeps them from getting bubbles in their blood, or something like that. Let's ask Steve. He's probably read about it in *Popular Science*."

"Okay, but first let's get a balloon and pull it on him. Let's don't tell anybody till after. Hot dog! Have you got any money? Balloons cost a quarter."

"Have I got any money?" Duncan groaned. "I owe Louie $12.50. But the balloons are free. They give 'em free to anybody who makes a contribution to the park band shell."

Gates sighed. "Big difference." Automatically they both looked up into the trees. Last year they had gathered quite a few balloons that had escaped into some easily climbed trees. "I don't see any loose ones," Gates said. "Anyway I've got to go home and do my homework so I can come back tonight. The hermit might come tonight."

"I doubt it. He doesn't have any electricity, so he probably goes to bed early. Tomorrow's when I get out of school early to do that TV thing with Joey. I sure hope tomorrow's not the day he comes, and you all get to do it without me."

Joey the Clown and the Pine Snake

A tiny red and white airplane hardly bigger than the museum station wagon taxied along the airstrip that lay between Highway 21 and the fairgrounds. Duncan, in the front seat of the station wagon beside his father, shifted the pine snake, which was peacefully coiled in a laundry bag, from his lap to the seat. He leaned out the window to watch the airplane, wishing he could go up in it sometime and circle around low over Charlotte. He'd like to see the hermit's shack from up there. The "shortcut" and the old bridge should be easy to spot. He'd found out from his father last night another reason the path was so wide. The driver for Morrison Barnes Market, who brought horsemeat to the Nature Museum, said he also made deliveries to the hermit.

Construction work was apparently under way at

the fairgrounds. The road was rutted with truck tracks, and a sign said DANGER—BLASTING.

In the back seat beside her owner, Mr. Casey, the cheetah sat, a tall passenger. She had to droop a little to take in everything that was going on out the window. Her stately head turned like an owl's as she noticed the airplane, kept tabs on the traffic in the left lane, disapproved—it seemed—of the silly rustling red and white plastic banners over the entrance, and studied the sign:

MECKLENBURG COUNTY FAIR

SHOWPLACE OF PROGRESS

AGRICULTURAL / INDUSTRIAL

Suddenly an explosion erupted. A geyser of dirt billowed up from the racetrack beyond the Exhibition Hall. As if she'd been shot at, the cheetah shrank to a crouch, quivering, her ears flat to her head. Mr. Casey grabbed her with both arms. "Quick, Dave, get them to quit the blasting!"

Mr. McKenna pulled up beside the WSOC-TV studio car and dashed into the fairground office. Mr. Casey softly scolded the cheetah and smoothed down the bristled hair on her neck.

Duncan's father was just coming out of the building when another blast occurred. This time the cheetah sprang into the front seat beside Duncan, one paw coming down on top of the laundry bag. The snake inside began to hiss and thrash around.

Duncan shoved the cheetah off the snake, and Mr. Casey made a dive for the handle of the open window, through which the cheetah would have leaped if the glass hadn't come up and held her back.

Mr. McKenna raced back into the office. Immediately from the back of the building a man ran out, got into a pickup truck, and spinning up dust, headed for the racetrack and the rock pile being blasted. Mr. Casey kept up a soothing conversation with the cheetah and rubbed her roughly, the sort of treatment she liked.

Duncan held the nervous snake like a pillow against his chest. His father watched through the window. "Bob, I can just see the headlines in tomorrow's *News*—'SPEEDWAY MASCOT ESCAPES.' Somebody'd be sure to organize a posse."

"Poor girl. She may have some lingering memory of her mother being shot by a safari hunter."

"More recent than that," Duncan blurted out. "Last week some stupid finks threw a cherry bomb at her."

"No wonder she's frightened. Come on back, girl." Mr. Casey pulled her over into the back seat. She leaned against him as he continued to talk to her and stroke her spotted hide. When she was relaxed and purring, they got out of the car, the cheetah on a short leash.

The exhibit area at the fairgrounds was a wide grassy corridor flanked by low, gray-painted barns with big open doors. Reading the labels on the barns, Duncan walked along, his hand on the cheetah's back, the snake bundled up and balanced on his shoulder. The barns were ready for occupancy, with straw in the stalls and pens, but the animals wouldn't arrive till fairtime in October.

In front of the cattle barn, three men were standing around a large aluminum suitcase. Duncan had been so busy with the snake that he hadn't had time to anticipate the meeting with Joey the Clown. So, when he saw him there, leaning on a railing at the cattle barn in his floppy black coat with the yellow elbow patch and the red flower sprouting out of his hatband—well, Duncan couldn't stop looking. Joey was the first TV personality he had ever seen in person. But Joey didn't notice Duncan; he was absorbed by something he was watching in one of the pens.

Duncan's father introduced Mr. Casey and Duncan to the three men from the studio. They were Mort, the director; Benny, the cameraman; and Price, the gopher guy—whatever that meant.

Price, the gopher guy, carried a shovel and a large paper bag. He was too big and shaggy-headed to resemble a neat little gopher. Duncan couldn't resist asking him the reason for the name.

"Gopher?" said Price grinning. "They call me that 'cause it's me they git to *go fer* whatever they need. I'm flunky, low man on the totem pole."

None of these men really looked at Duncan as they were introduced. They smiled and nodded, but they didn't offer to shake hands. Their eyes were fixed on the slightly moving bag in Duncan's arms. They were more polite to Mr. Casey, and they admired the docile cheetah. Then they began a discussion of the shooting.

Duncan tied a knot in the top of the laundry bag and set it down in a clump of grass beside the barn. Joey's arms were hooked over the top railing of the pen, and his white gloved hands hung limp. Duncan looked carefully over the straw in the pen, but he couldn't find even a spider to look at. After a few moments Joey said, "Isn't that the fattest pig you ever did see?"

Duncan stared at the empty pen and beyond it to the other pens and stalls. There wasn't a pig in the place. He looked back at Joey, beginning to laugh on the inside. "Uuuuuuuuuuh . . ." As he gathered his wits together he took in the whole spectrum of Joey's face, his bright blue eyes with four little birdfoot tracks beside them, red nose, white smiling mouth, and the rest of it plain, a normally smudged hobo's face. "Uuuuuuuuuh . . . That's a pig? I uuuuuuuuh, I thought it said CATTLE on a sign out there."

"It did? Well, I declare"—Joey pulled his pockets wrong side out—"I must of left my specs at home." His white-gloved fingers came through a rip in a side seam of the coat as he fumbled in an inside pocket. "Leastwise I think I did. If I ever had any." He did a few slow sidesteps down the railing till he was close to Duncan. Then in a confidential tone he said, "Don't it look somewhat more like a pig than a cow to you? You know, sometimes you can't believe what you read."

Duncan's chin mashed down on his fist on the wooden railing in an effort to keep back the wild grin that wanted to wash out all over his face. He frowned into the empty pen and then nodded. "That's a curly tail, all right. But pigs don't have horns. I know that."

Joey scratched under the brim of his rumpled top hat. "That bothered me too. It sure did. But I'll tell you for true, it don't really matter. What got me right here"—he laid his hand over the loop of his red necktie—"about him out there"—he gazed fondly into the pen—"was them perdy white eyelashes. It put me to mind of Uncle Louie."

"I have a friend named Louie," Duncan said.

Joey nodded, and the red flower on its wire stem nodded too. "You know, kiddo, when I was a little boy I used to have a lot of things, like marbles and skates and whistles and whittling knives, and you know, there's none of 'em around any more. They all got lost. But I never lost a friend."

Joey's arms flopped over the railing again. His black long-tailed coat hunched up high over his shoulders and covered up his ears as he rested his chin on the railing. "Nope, I never lost a friend. A friend's a friend. You go through troubles together."

"Louie's that kind of a friend. I lost his paper-route money, and do you know what he said?"

"What'd he say?"

"It was thirteen dollars and he said it was okay, it was partly his fault, and I only needed to pay him back half of it. But it really was my fault, Joey. I put it in my shirt pocket, and it fell out.

"Did you stand on your head?"

"No, I was just crawling down this place. Have you ever seen a lizard doing push-ups?"

Joey grinned and turned around, so that his back was against the railing. He looked up at the roof of the barn. "Now there's a happy memory I got." He looked over at Duncan and chuckled. "Used to be a little fence lizard. Most every day he'd stand up there on my stack of firewood and look me in the eye and push up and down like that. He was my friend. So you were doin' push-ups when you lost the money."

"I wasn't exactly *doing* push-ups. I was just pushing up so I could see in this window."

"What'd you see?"

"A bed with an army blanket and a black stove and a long-barreled gun and a whole, whole lot of magazines. We didn't know somebody lived there. We thought kids built it. There were lots of dogs in a pen there—puppies and big ones with long frizzled hair over their eyebrows and on their ears. They're Afghans, my dad says."

"And that's where you lost Louie's money."

"Yes, I guess so."

"Well, you kin just git your daddy to take you back to look fer it."

"No, I can't. See, if my dad took me over there—" How had he gotten so far in spilling all this? Duncan frowned down at the straw on the floor of the pen. Everything had just seemed to slip out as if Joey were an old friend and ought to know. "If my dad took me over there, he'd tell the hermit it was all a mistake and not let him shoot me or anything, but I can't tell my dad."

Joey was no longer gazing up at the cobwebs on the rafters. But he still slouched, his elbow on the fence, his head on his hand. His eyes were a greenish blue, and his real mouth as well as the big white painted one smiled. "Now you got me all confoosed," he said slowly, scratching his head. "You gotta begin again and tell me slow, so's I kin understand about you and Louie and all them curly-headed dogs."

So Duncan began to try to make sense to Joey. He had more friends than just Louie, he said. There were six friends, and they always did important things together. And so everybody wanted to help get Louie's money back.

It all came out. How the bearded hermit, whom Duncan guessed to be about seven feet tall, was known to visit the Festival in the park every year, how Duncan and his friends were "on call" all week waiting for him to appear, hoping it would be after school or on Saturday or Sunday, so they could speed over to his shack and find the money. A paratrooper named Fred was keeping a lookout too, but Fred didn't know about the raid. He just thought Duncan was curious to see a freak, a man that tall with a beard that long and that strange a looking pack of dogs.

Duncan's attempt at explanation was cut short by a call from Mort. "We're ready, Joey."

Joey took off his hat, scruffled up his sparse reddish hair, and put it back on. "All right, come along, kiddo. They've got us a job to do. It's only civilized everybody should work some of the time. But while I'm workin' I'm goin' to be thinkin' about you and Louie and *him* and them silky-haired dogs."

The filming would begin with Joey and the snake. Mr. Casey would take the cheetah out beside the high fence where they had strung the wire. He'd get her used to the short leash slipping along the tight wire. Then with the lure of some hamburger meat, they'd get some good running shots. To make sure that the goodwill and patience of the blasting crew held out, Duncan's father would go over to the blasting site and talk to the men there.

When Mr. Casey and his father had gone, Duncan picked up the heavy bag full of snake and listened to instructions from Mort. Mort clicked his ball-point pen as he explained what he hoped for from the snake. He and Benny and Price all backed up a few steps when Duncan undid the laundry bag.

Duncan caught the snake behind the head and brought it out swinging; its thick black and white body lashed back and forth until he got it securely gathered in a bundle against his chest.

"My goodness, my goodness, my goodness!" Joey ducked behind the cameraman. He peeked out around his elbow. "Good gracious, kiddo, that's a snake!" Duncan grinned. It was fun being around Joey, even if he was afraid of snakes.

According to plan, Duncan lay down behind a bale of hay in the doorway of the poultry barn. "Shoot," the director said. The camera began to whir. Duncan pushed the snake's head up over the bale of hay. Little by little he eased it up until it began to move on its own. It crawled over the top of the hay and down to the dirt floor. Then it took off for the tall grass.

"Cut," said Mort. "That was good. Catch your snake, Duncan. Say, how fast can this thing travel?"

"Not too fast to catch. But anyway, she's tame. She won't try to get away unless she gets scared. Just don't move up on her suddenly."

"I *promise!*" said Benny, adjusting the camera strap over his shoulder. "You tell her the same thing about me."

Duncan had to laugh at these three grown men, all of them so awed by an ordinary pine snake that kids at the Nature Museum handled every day.

"Don't worry about this snake," Duncan said. "She's tired, even. She's digesting a baby chick from this morning."

"Yeccccck!" The saggy lines of Benny's St. Bernard dog face all turned upside down. Mort cleared his throat. Price bulged out his cheeks and began to sway to the left. Just before falling flat, he propped himself up on the shovel.

"Price, did you plant the daisies?" Mort asked.

"Yup."

"I see. And Joey's all set." He tapped his clipboard with the ball-point pen. "Duncan, aim your snake so he'll crawl down toward Joey there. You're sure he won't bite."

"Positive."

Joey leaned against the barn, under a sign that said POULTRY. Beside him was the newly planted clump of daisies. "She loves me, she loves me not, she loves me, she loves me not." One by one Joey pulled the petals off a daisy. Mort looked through his viewer at Joey and then spoke to Benny, who set the camera on a tripod, adjusting the legs down to short. "Give us a two shot, medium, and follow the action. All right, Duncan, let your snake loose. Shoot."

Duncan put the snake on the ground. Benny crouched behind the camera, and the whirring began. The snake turned her attention to the new sound, flapping her tongue. Then slowly, with obvious fascination, she began to weave in on the camera, her head high. "Hey, wait a minute. She's headed wrong," Benny complained. "Call it, Mort. She's not going right. She's coming at *me*. Come on, Mort. I'm allergic."

But Mort didn't call for a cut. "Please, Benny. Stay with it. Don't panic. This'll be good."

The snake moved steadily toward Benny, and Benny's whine became more and more jittery. His face was hidden behind the view finder, but his ears turned bright red. "What you trying to do to me, Mort? Bring on a heart attack?"

"Okay, cut. Great shot, Benny. Get the snake, Duncan, quick before Benny has a stroke."

Throughout all this, Joey had been absorbed in the daisies. He picked another, smelled it, and then began again, "She loves me, she loves me not. . . ."

For the next scene Mort wanted the camera on the other side of Joey, so the snake couldn't be lured away from Joey by the sound of it. Joey crossed his ankle over his knee. The lacing of his high-top tennis shoe dangled, and the tongue flapped over. He put a daisy behind his ear and tied the shoe halfway down. The tongue still hung over. Several times he rolled it up and pinched it, but it wouldn't stay rolled. Finally with his fingers like a pair of scissors Joey pretended to cut it off. He put the "flap" he had "cut off" into a pocket in his yellow vest. Then he snapped his green suspenders, sighed happily and plucked another daisy.

Price set up the tripod for Benny in the new location. "What's the matter, Benny, you got the shakes?"

"Ha! You would too if a boa constrictor had just slithered up on you."

"It's only a pine snake," Duncan said.

"Pine snake, fine snake, it's all the same. I told you, I'm allergic."

"All right, Benny," Mort said crisply. "That was magnificent back there. What do you want—a medal? Shoot."

Duncan put the snake on the ground and snapped his fingers. With a jerk it started off through the tall grass close to the barn. Joey kept talking to himself and pulling off petals. Duncan chewed his knuckle, wondering what would happen next. He knew Joey was afraid of snakes, and yet here he was, leaning back against the barn like a limp dummy, as if he didn't know what was crawling up on him. Surely, out of the corner of his eye he could see. . . .

"She loves me, she loves me not. . . ."

Benny was down on one knee, intensely filming the route of the snake. At a small opening between the barn and the tails of Joey's black coat, the snake hesitated. It looked up at Joey with a flipping tongue. Then it nudged under the flap of his coat and crawled behind him. Duncan bit hard on his knuckle. He wanted so badly to reassure Joey, to tell him not to be afraid, that this was a good snake. But he had been told that nobody was supposed to talk except the director.

"That guy's got nerves of steel," Mort said in a low voice to Benny.

For some reason, maybe the brightness of the afternoon sun on the other side of Joey, the snake turned around and began to crawl back through the tunnel between Joey and the barn. When the head began to come out where the tail had not yet all disappeared, the director clicked his pen and whispered, "Okay, Joey. Get ready for the business."

Joey dropped a petal slowly as he looked up toward the sky, frowning as if he thought something unusual was going on behind his back. His hand stayed poised in the air over the daisy, the little finger curved up. Slowly his gaze moved down and around to the right. He took a look at the loop of snake, a foot and a half or two feet, that was visible on the right of him, and then with his little finger still cocked up over the daisy, he moved his head slowly to the left. Almost as if he hated to do it, he glanced down, coming face to face with the lifted head of the snake.

"Hold it, Joey, that's beautiful!" Mort purred.

Joey held it, his hand still hanging limp in midair, his painted face frozen in a comical exaggeration of disbelief.

"Cut. Duncan, go get your snake quick."

Duncan got down on his knees to gather up the snake. "I thought you were afraid of snakes, Joey."

"I tell you true, kiddo, I been sittin' here with this one so long now we've got to be pretty good buddies. But my natural feelin's about snakes is usually to go in the other direction."

For the next scene Mort wanted a shot of the snake looking fierce and coiled to strike. When a pine snake is threatened, it has a phony way of trying to scare off the enemy. To get this one coiled and looking dangerous, Duncan rattled in its face the paper bag Price had brought the clump of daisies in. It worked. The snake's tail shivered, setting the grass to rustling; its head reared back over the pile of coils; it hissed like an angry swan and seemed ready to lunge with its full weight. But it didn't. Instead it slunk down into the grass.

Benny got shots of the initial blustering and then more of the snake going fast through the grass and down the road. Duncan ran up ahead of her, and she stopped. After a bit of soft talk, she let herself be picked up and put back in the laundry bag.

Benny followed the snake shots with one of Joey falling all over himself in an effort to get up. He got his knee on his red necktie, which pinned him to the ground for a while. Then he ran like crazy, his coattails flying and his arms waving disjointedly. These shots would be interspersed with some scenes taken at the fair the previous year.

Now Mort was ready for the cheetah and Mr. Casey to come back. They were out by the twelve-foot fence, relaxing under a big oak tree. Mort put his fingers to his mouth and proved that he could really whistle.

Joey and the Cheetah

Mr. Casey, who had been lying in the grass with the top of his head butted up against the cheetah's back, heard Mort's shrill whistle and stood up. It wasn't so simple to arouse the cheetah. Mr. Casey tugged at her collar, but she didn't seem to mind having her neck stretched. With his arms around her stomach he lifted her, but she sagged down again. Duncan, as he watched from in front of the poultry barn, could imagine the deep-down purr that must be rumbling forth from that contented cat. How would they ever get her running? But finally she got up, stretched down in a low bow, and came along like an old dog on a leash.

Mort liked her. He patted her between the ears. Price picked up the aluminum camera case and the shovel. Benny carried the tripod over his shoulder and the camera around his neck as they all went back toward the front office by the Exhibition Hall.

While Mort explained what he wanted from everybody in this next sequence, the cheetah lay down by the front tire of the pickup truck. Duncan sat beside her and scratched her stomach. She yawned, and her long pink tongue curled up.

Her paws were a reminder that she was no ordinary cat. Most of the cat family have retractable claws; their paws are as smooth as mittens. But the claws of the cheetah were always ready for use. Although they were worn dull at the tip, this old cat could still, if she had the chance, bring down a full-grown antelope galloping.

"Duncan, stand up here. I've got a small part here for you," Mort said. Wow! Duncan got up quickly. "You're part of the crowd, Duncan, and you've struck up a friendship with Joey."

It would begin with Joey and Duncan sitting on the tailgate of the pickup truck. "Benny, I want a cover shot of that sign at the entrance, then the Exhibition Hall and the truck with the boy and the clown. Pan left to include the airstrip. Time it to get the plane landing." He squinted up into the sky. "It's coming in now. Make it about twenty seconds' duration." Benny nodded and went off with the camera and tripod. "Casey, I hope you can get that cheetah awake for the next scene."

"No trouble. She loves trucks. She'll think she's going for a ride."

Mort nodded, but he looked skeptically at the cheetah as she lay with her ear against the dusty hubcap. When Benny came back, he set up the camera facing the rear of the truck. Joey and Duncan sat on the tailgate. Joey swung his legs, so Duncan did too. "First scene all you do is talk to each other. Don't look at the camera, Duncan. Not even once. Okay? All right, shoot, Benny."

"Look over there," Joey said, pointing to the red and white airplane that had just landed. "That's the little plane that takes you up over the top of the city."

Duncan said he'd like to go up in it sometime. "It costs some money to go up," Joey said. "Let's see if I've got any money." He began searching through his pockets.

"I don't have any money," Duncan said. "I owe Louie thirteen dollars, you remember."

Joey nodded. "Yes, I remember. That's too bad." The flower bounced up and down.

"Where'd you get that flower on your hat, Joey?"

Joey giggled. "Would you believe it? A girl scout gave it to me."

"Cut. Fine, you two. All right, next I want a medium two shot to include the top of the truck. While you two are talking I want the cheetah to appear up there on the cab roof. You sure she'll do it, Casey?"

"I told you she will. She was raised in a truck—rode all over the African veld in one."

Mr. Casey was right. With very little urging the cheetah hopped up on the hood of the truck and

98

from there leaped to the cab roof. Her claws clattered on the metal.

The camera caught it all as Duncan and Joey carried on more talk about the airplane, seemingly unaware that a big spotted cat had appeared behind them.

"Cut." Mort wiped his forehead with his handkerchief. "Beautiful," he said, looking up at the cheetah who sat tall and expectant, ready for a ride, her eyes scanning the distance. The black tip of her tail tapped the roof. The leash hung down from her collar as if she'd escaped from somewhere. But she wasn't really loose; a long extension on the leash allowed Mr. Casey to hold her without being caught in the picture.

In the next scene Duncan pointed out the airstrip as Mort told him to do and said he was going to go get a close look at that airplane. Then he hopped down off the tailgate of the truck.

"Now come on here, big cheetah," Mort said. "Stand up and get your tail on down here. Joey, this may be a wait—dern cat's half asleep again." Duncan could hear her purring from where he stood beside Benny. "Casey, talk to her. Get her down for a look at Joey. Ready, Joey. Shoot."

"Come on, speedy girl," Mr. Casey urged. "Come on down. Be a good girl." He whistled softly, but she ignored him.

Joey yawned, and his shoulders drooped. His feet

stopped swinging. With his white-gloved hands he reached down and picked up his feet by the floppy tongues of his old tennis shoes. He laid them out straight on the tailgate. Then he leaned into the side of the truck. His hat fell off. Slowly he slid down till he was flat on his back and seemingly asleep. His big white mouth made fishlike *O*'s as he breathed.

"Cut. Casey, how're we going to get that lazy animal down there with Joey? Price, what have you got she might like?"

"Cigarettes?" Price patted his shirt pocket and grinned.

Duncan found in his pocket the crinkly paper and crumbs from a package of peanut-butter crackers. "Maybe this will do it." He climbed up on the side of the truck and gave the cheetah a sniff; then he dropped the paper near Joey in the bed of the truck. The cheetah's ears perked forward, and she stood up.

"Shoot." The whirring began again as the big cat hopped gracefully down, put her nose up close to Joey's ear and sniffed the peanut-butter-cracker paper. "Beautiful!" Mort purred. "Cat, you're the greatest. You, too, Duncan."

Joey stirred, scratched his nose and sat up, folding his legs up under his elbows. The cheetah ambled over and sat on her haunches beside Joey, gazing off into the distance. Joey squinted up at the sky. "What was that you whiskered in my ear, kiddo? Did you git to see the little airplane up close? I tell you true, fact is, my eyes went to sleep on me, and I forgot to watch."

Mort was ecstatic. "Gorgeous," he murmured, his ball-point pen clicking. "This cat's a doll. Hold on, Joey, drag it out. This is incredible!"

Joey leaned into the cheetah, and she swayed to the right. They both swayed back to the left and then back to the right. Back and forth they rocked. "Unbelievable," Mort said, "unbelievable. Get ready, Joey. Hold on, Benny, Zoom in on Joey when he sees it's the cat and panics."

Joey hummed a tune, and the cheetah purred. He reached out and patted her paw. "Someday I'm going to get me a ride in that little airplane and have a look down on the tops of those Charlotte skyscrapers. What a sight! Me up there like a bird with my wings out." Joey spread his arms wide. The right arm fell across the cheetah's shoulders, and he gave her a hug. Then he looked her in the face.

"Hold it, Benny." Mort's ball-point pen clicked like a summer cricket. "All right, Joey—comes the realization." Joey continued to beam at the cheetah. "Comes the realization, Joey. . . . For Pete's sake, man, react! Now is the time to get scared!"

Joey appeared not to hear Mort. His smile got broader. "Mercy me," he said, touching the cheetah's spotted chin.

"Joey," Mort pleaded frantically. "You're supposed to be scared. You gotta project shock like we planned."

"You know, the joke's on me," Joey said softly to the cheetah. "I thought you were a boy."

Mort went limp. The ball-point pen dropped into the dirt. The camera continued to whir as Joey touched the cheetah's round ears and nodded. "You suppose I should get my glasses changed?"

Benny looked at Mort for instructions. Mort's arms hung at his sides, one finger hooked through the hole at the top of the clipboard. A baffled look puckered his face.

The cheetah sniffed Joey's cheek, and Joey smiled as if he'd been kissed. "Thing I like best about the county fair," he said, looking just over Benny's head, "is the nice kind of folks you get to meet there."

No one moved for a long quiet moment. Then Mort came to as if a gust of wind had hit him. He fumbled the papers in his clipboard.

"Hey, Mort, how long you want I should hold on?"

Mort didn't look up. "Cut," he said. He filled two pages with his rapid writing while everyone stood around saying nothing. "That'll do," he said finally and strode off toward the studio car.

Benny called after him, "What d'ya mean, 'That'll do'?"

"That'll do. No chase. Let's go home."

Duncan ran to catch up with Mort. "You mean the cheetah isn't going to run on the wire?"

Mort slowed down and put his pen in an inside

pocket. "Thing about working with that clown is you never know what he's going to do next. Plan a straight scene when he's himself, regular, you know —fine. We understand each other. But get him into that crazy Joey skin, and he's somebody else, he's Joey the Clown, and he does what comes into his half-witted head. But what gets me is it usually works! This guy has an instinct for the great line on the spot." Mort shook his head. "Like this—today. Instead of the funny business we plan, he pulls off the greatest promotion scene you could possibly dream up." He opened the front door of the studio station wagon and got in. He rolled the window down and grinned at Duncan. " 'Thing I like best about the county fair is the nice folks you get to meet there.' " He sighed. "Beautiful!"

Mort stayed behind the wheel with his contented look while Price and Benny packed the camera and tripod into the aluminum case. Duncan's father had returned from the blasting site soon enough to have seen the final filming but not to have heard what was said. Mr. Casey explained to him what had happened that made the running shots of the cheetah unnecessary. The cheetah was now eating the hamburger—and the plastic bag it was in.

Where was Joey? Duncan walked back to the truck and found him still on the tailgate, stretched out as if asleep. He sat up yawning. "I was hopin' you'd come find me, kiddo," he said. "I been ponderin' what you told me. Yes, sir, I'd sure myself like a look at them funny-lookin' hairy-faced dogs." He leaned his head back and stared up at the sky. The little airplane was letting out a trail of smoke, but Joey didn't mention it. "I wish I was young again and could take up some more adventures. Now, if I was young again, I'd just slip onto my bicycle and ride around with you boys."

"Have you got a bicycle, Joey?"

Joey tapped his fingers together and frowned. "I had me one named Bluebird, but it must of got lost. Now if I was young again, I'd go out yonder there and help you boys find that money, and take a peek at them dogs in the pen and pat their noses, and then I'd high-tail it out of there before the big fella got back." There was a big sad smile on Joey's face.

Duncan couldn't very well invite Joey to come along with them, but he'd have liked to. He had a funny picture of how conspicuous they'd be, riding bikes with Joey the Clown. Every kid along the route would get on his bike and follow.

"You know what's next best to real adventurin'?" Joey's legs swung lazily off the end of the tailgate. Duncan expected him to say reading, as teachers and parents always did, but Joey said, "Dreaming. If I only knew when the raid was going to be, so I could dream about it at the right time. That's the best kind of dreamin'. . . . Like when those fellows went up to the moon in that funny-lookin' trailer, I dreamed I was there, how nothin' would stay down, and my necktie floated out front like this, and my hat went driftin' off with my flashlight."

Duncan smiled. Joey was such a nut. It didn't take much to make him happy. But he was probably a lot smarter than he looked. He might not be able to follow instructions, but Mort appreciated him. He'd kept his job at the TV station a long time. And also, Duncan reminded himself, a clown is a clown only when he is dressed as a clown. Joey was somebody else too. But when you were around Joey, you got under his spell. That's what Mort meant. There was no other way to explain it. Like when Joey pretended there was a pig in the pen, you wouldn't want to embarrass him by saying, "Come off it, Joey, there's not any pig in that pen." Automatically it was fun to go along with Joey's games. "Joey, you can dream about us finding the money and escaping if you want to."

Joey dropped his chin onto his fist. "Problem is *when*. Could you call me on the telly-phone?"

That wouldn't work. "We'll be in an awful hurry, Joey. I'd probably forget."

Joey fumbled through his pockets. He brought out a piece of paper and a pencil. On the paper he wrote J O E Y in sprawling letters. He bit his tongue as he wrote. "I also know how to write my two telly-phone numbers. This is my TV number, and this is where I live." He gave the paper to Duncan.

"I might forget. . . ." Also how would he be able

to explain to his mother, making a phone call like that? She'd start asking questions.

Joey seemed to be a mind reader. He brought out a dime from his pocket. "You kin call me from the fillin' station if you forget to at home."

Duncan looked at the dime, reluctant to be pinned down by Joey and one of his crazy games. Joey tipped his head to one side and the bird's-foot creases at the corners of his blue green eyes made little humps in the white paint. "A favor for a friend," he said.

"Okay, Joey, I'll call you." He put the paper and the dime in his pocket.

The Happening and the Rope Bridge

Louie wasn't laughing at THE HAPPENING, but almost everybody else was. Louie's long jaw, so good for making crazy faces, was firm with concentration as if he was searching for a hidden meaning behind the surface nonsense of these steel trees decorated with objects that jittered, bounced, and blinked in their little orbits.

Louie was so absorbed by this galaxy of strange motorized gadgets that he didn't even notice Duncan, Gates, and Steve till they surrounded him. "Ye gods, would you look," he said, getting back into his usual self. He pointed with a twitching finger at the revolving centerpiece, a toilet with butterflies coming out of it.

"Here comes Monroe," Gates said. "I know he'll have a fit over that."

Then Monroe spotted the toilet with the butterflies, and he about fell apart laughing. "I dare you to go see if it works," Gates chortled.

Steve grabbed him by the arm again. "Don't suggest it, Gates. He might just do it." But Monroe said indignantly that he wasn't *that* mixed up.

Louie was examining the bulletin board that explained how THE HAPPENING had happened to be built. There were pictures of the sixteen artists who had put it together. "When I grow up," Louie told Duncan, "I'm going to be a dimensional artist, and I'll go all over the country putting up displays for festivals and playgrounds and parks. They won't all be goofy either. Some will be permanent—great works of art."

He grinned and changed the subject. He had just talked to Fred. "He said if we wanted to see the hermit so bad we ought to just go over to his place and pretend we wanted to buy a puppy."

"Yeh, sure, and get arrested for peeping in windows."

"Also for trespassing, vagrancy, attempted vandalism, et cetera," Louie said. "I sure hope your dad's right, and he does come here. Saturday would be best. Otherwise we'll just have to forget the whole thing."

"*I* can't forget it. I'll have a lot of yardwork to do to earn twelve fifty."

"It's only six dollars you owe me, Dunc. We did it together."

"That's what I told Joey you said."

"You told Joey the Clown?"

"Yeh, I told him. I said you were so bull-headed you insisted it was half your fault."

"It is."

"No, it isn't."

"Come on, you guys," Steve called. "Let's go try out the rope bridge."

The rope bridge had been built for the Festival by the boy scouts of Troop 55 of the Myers Park Presbyterian Church. Made completely of rope, it looped over the water between the mainland and the island. The idea was to walk across on the center rope, holding the two side railings for support. Up and down between the center rope and these railings, more rope was knotted like a retaining net to help keep the traveler aboard. The problem was that the bridge was a real bouncer. It pitched around like an oriole's nest in the wind. Louie said, though, that the boys who had built it had practiced so much that they could run across it like Tarzan. But the ordinary pedestrian had better watch out.

A line of teen-age boys and girls waited for turns. The shrieking and hamming it up that went on was something to watch. The long-haired girls would flop into the arms of the boys when the rope walk was over as if they'd been through torture, and the boys loved it. High school boys were sure crazy about girls.

Duncan, Louie, Steve, Gates, and Monroe finally

got up to the platform. Louie had to make a speech. "Friends," he said in a quivering voice, "on the rocky road of life I have learned some valuable lessons, which I would pass along to all who would follow in my footsteps. The last time I ventured forth on this famous bridge of many ropes I suffered greatly. Yes, friends, I almost tossed my cookies to the fish below." He hung his head. "This time"—he made a flourish with his lanky arm and pointed to the heavens—"I shall use a new technique. I shall glide like a tightrope walker." His friends chuckled at his usual verbosity, and the boy scout in charge of the operation leaned back on the wooden railing, his arms crossed over his red kerchief, and grinned indulgently. "Remember, my little buddies," said Louie, smiling down at a bunch of younger children who eyed him respectfully, "it's the motion in the middle that gets you in the gut!" He clapped his hand over his stomach and rolled out his tongue. There was a rustle of titters from his audience.

For a moment then Louie rubbed his hands briskly together, his shoulders hunched up high under his ears. Then he rose on tiptoe, hummed a little tune, and swooped off. He had gone a third of the distance when the rhythm of the bridge caught up with him and shattered his choir director's poise.

"Help," he shrieked as the rope dropped out from under and a horizontal wobble heaved him into the side ropes, causing his feet to tangle with each other. Down he came; it was perfect. He didn't catch hold of the side ropes; he just folded up, and his whole body slipped through the ropes. One knee caught around the center rope. His arms thrashed madly, and his hair skimmed the water.

"I knew he'd flub it," the boy scout said. "All right, wise guy, you're holding up the works."

Louie straightened out his leg and fell headfirst into the lake. He plowed back to shore, his hair matted with mud, his shirttail clinging to his pants.

"Bravo, Louie. Your turn, Monroe," Steve said.

"You've got leaves all over you, Louie," Gates said, pulling soggy leaves off Louie's shirt.

"But I'm cool." Louie grinned blissfully.

Monroe came back complaining that nobody had watched him. "It hardly wobbled at all."

"That's because you're such a flea weight," Steve told him. "By the way, where's Marshall?"

"His snake is having babies. He's at the museum," Duncan said. "Here I go."

He rushed out on the ropes with short quick steps, the opposite of Louie's long swooping ones. But they didn't cut down on the bounce. He fell into the net, and a side-to-side roll was added to the up-and-down heaving. He felt like a raft in white-water rapids. His stomach collided with his heart and lungs, as it did in the elevator at the Doctors' Building. He made it to the island and back, staggered down the steps, and flopped on the grass, reeling. There had to be a trick to that bridge. Sometime

when there weren't any people around, he'd practice till he got the knack of it.

He thought about Marshall's snake having babies, and that reminded him about the turtle, a plain ordinary green slider, that was always laying eggs out of season. Grandpa, the custodian, was going to save him some eggs if he could get them before the other turtles broke them. Possibly they were fertilized and would hatch. He hopped up off the grass. "I'm going up to the museum. I want to check on something. See you later."

"Alligator," Monroe added.

Monroe always said that. "No, Monroe, you're wrong. It's a turtle."

Marshall, the Turtle Authority

As Duncan opened the door to the Animal Room, it struck him immediately that something unusual was happening. The room was full of people not talking, but facing toward the turtle pool. Because of all the people, Duncan couldn't see the semicircular pool, but he could hear the water trickling down over layers of flat rock. Two big picture windows on each side of the pool overlooked a woodsy deer pen and bird sanctuary. Over the pool hung a stuffed giant sea turtle. Around the edges of the room were aquariums of fish; glass-fronted cages containing small animals and birds; and terrariums with snakes entwined in small trees, soaking in water dishes, or lying still on the white stones. Under a glass dome on a pillar was a furry brown mouse-sized tarantula, a Texas spider someone had donated as an exhibit. Another new donation was a colony of honeybees in a simulated hollow tree with an opening to the outdoors. Through the windows in the tree you could watch the honey-making bees all bumbling around on their honeycomb.

But people weren't watching the bees or the animals either. They were listening to a man at the edge of the pool who had a lot to say about turtles —a ruddy-faced, dusty-haired, purple-shirted orator. His back to the green parrot's cage, he looked his audience over and said expansively, "Yes, siree bob, them snappers grow tremendous. Three hunnert pounds some of 'em git. Live to be four hunnert year old."

Bull! Duncan said to himself. In the first place, no turtle on record ever lived more than one hundred years. Common snappers like the one in the pool never got bigger than 30 pounds in the wild either. Even the largest *alligator* snapper ever caught weighed just 219 pounds.

Duncan's friend Marshall was sitting on the edge of the pool across from the burly man in the white-and-purple striped shirt. Marshall's jaw was clamped tight. Over his face he had slicked his stupid look. The *real* Marshall had the detached, level-eyed, intelligent look of the noted biologist he was going to be when he grew up. Now though his light blue eyes were half closed and glazed over with the dullness of a snake's eyes before it sheds its skin.

At the sight of Duncan, Marshall came to life. He

rolled his eyes up to the ceiling and then swooped them back at the man in the striped shirt. Apparently this "lecture" had been going on for some time. One of the things that really bugged Marshall, who had read every book about reptiles in the museum library, was the way some know-nothings liked to spout off a lot of rot about reptiles, especially snakes, just to scare people and make themselves look brave.

"Yup," the man said, surveying the crowd of mostly mothers and children. "Snap them jaws down on a person's leg, and he won't let go till sundown." With his elbow Marshall nudged Duncan who had come up behind him. "Yup, I've seen snappers twice that big in the Pee Dee River."

"World's record," Marshall drawled out of the side of his mouth. Then in a whisper he asked Duncan if the hermit had been seen. Duncan shook his head. "I didn't think so or you'd have said so, and we'd be on our way. I got my flat tire fixed," Marshall whispered.

The man sat down on the edge of the pool and clasped his hairy hands around his knee. His fingernails were dirty. For a moment his restless eye caught Duncan's, then veered off to gather in the eyes of the whole room. He unclasped his hands and pointed to the two baby alligators and the different kinds of turtles which he referred to as "green," "mud," "leatherback," "cooter," and "growed-up dime-store variety." He was interrupted once by the green parrot, in the cage just behind his shoulder, who said in a high sweet lady's voice, "Hello." He didn't answer the parrot, but several children did.

The shiny black eyes of the large snapper took in the motion of the man's flipping hands. Its neck, made of tough elephant hide, stretched up, and its throat bulged in and out like an old man's Adam's apple. Its shell resembled a three-dimensional topographical map with slatelike peaks and gullies. "That kind's not bad eatin'," the man said. "I've kilt many a snapper back home."

A small child with Popsicle drips on his white T shirt, whose chin barely came up to the pool's edge, asked timidly, "How?"

The man rubbed the palms of his hands together. "How'd I kill 'em you want to know? Well, I tell you, boy, you can shoot 'em, or you kin ax their heads off, but my buddy and me did it another way once. Caught a snapper on a line and hauled him up on the bank. Man, was he red-eyed!"

The people nearest to him backed away when he went into a reenactment of the killing. "My buddy grabbed him by the lower jaw with a pair of pliers, like *thith*." He caught his own lower jaw between his thumb and third finger, which put a lisp into his speech. "Caught him thith-a-way and yanked hard while I thtepped my foot on hith back." He took his hand out of his mouth and continued, his eyes darting from face to face. "Then I got me a fishin' line doubled twice over, and I got him around the neck and strangled him till he was dead."

The man was flushed in the face and breathing fast as if he'd just gone through the execution again. He laced his fingers through his thick dusty hair. Then he settled back on the ledge and began a dissertation on the soft-shell, which he called a "leatherback." The black eyes of the snapper followed his pointing fingers.

Duncan nudged Marshall, and Marshall nudged back. What they both wished was that the dangling hands would dangle just a bit farther down toward the alert old snapper. And when he caught a few of the man's fingers, Duncan would say with a pitiful face, "Too bad, sir, but he won't let go till sundown . . . unless it thunders, of course."

Duncan's grin was about to shake loose into mad laughter when the man pointed excitedly. "Oh, oh, there's gonna be a fight. That little green job's fixin' for a fight."

Marshall gave Duncan another jab with his elbow and rolled his eyes to the ceiling. Marshall's face was sternly set against laughing out loud.

In the pool a slider about five inches across was reaching forward in the water, vigorously vibrating its long claws in the face of the larger slider, the one that was always laying eggs. Everyone around the pool jostled for position to watch the fight that would surely develop. "That little green half-pint's astin' for it. He's just astin' to get them dandy fingernails of his clipped and half his leg bit off too. Smart aleck there had better quit teasin'!"

Now Marshall cleared his throat and said, "Uuuu-uuuuh . . . ," which Duncan knew meant that the time had come. Marshall was going to speak up.

"Uuuuuuh . . . ," he repeated, his voice low and nasal. "Excuse me, sir, but there's not going to be any fight."

There was a rustle among the listeners as heads shifted toward Marshall. Water trickled over rocks in the pool, and from the weasel's cage came the squeal of the play wheel. The man straightened up to his full height and rubbed his jaw, which jutted to one side. It made a rasping sound. His eyes seemed to darken and his face to redden as he frowned across the pool at Marshall, this impudent kid who had challenged him. It was a spooky look.

Marshall didn't fidget. He could even talk to Mr. Suber, the principal, without fidgeting. "Uuuuuuh," he said in his nasal monotone. "That smaller one's a male Troost's turtle, commonly called a slider. He's just trying to get the attention of the female. It's the normal courtship pattern that usually takes place in spring, but since these turtles are out of their normal environment, their mating cycle is mixed up, and this behavior goes on all year around. It is probably the effect of the sunlamp, which has given him too much vitamin D."

No one moved till the man did. He hitched up his pants, gave a snort, and said, "Not all smart alecks is turtles." Then he took hold of a meek little girl, who had apparently come with him, and shouldered his

way through the crowd and out the door.

It happened so fast that everyone just stared at the closed door for a while. Then the flying squirrel and the ferret joined the weasel in spinning their wheels. Joe the crow began to call for Grandpa. The old snapper crawled off his rock and splashed in the water.

The green male slider still quivered his long claws in the face of the large female. A lady with two small children asked Marshall, "Is that turtle really just flirting?"

"Yes," said Marshall.

"Maybe you can tell me something else. I had an argument with my sister. She says that at St. Simon's Island last year she saw sea turtles teaching the baby ones how to run to the sea."

Marshall laughed. "More *likely* they were trying to *eat* the babies," he said. "You can sit down by one of those big sea turtles while she's laying eggs and put all the eggs in a bucket while she watches you, and she doesn't care. She fills up the empty hole with sand out of instinct."

"I told my sister turtles didn't have any maternal instinct," the lady said, patting the heads of her two children.

"That's right. All reptiles are like that." Marshall showed her the garter snake that had just had babies.

It was in a terrarium on the window ledge, a tiny woodland scene with moss and ferns rooted in leaf mold. The mother garter snake, about eighteen inches long with yellow horizontal stripes, was draped like Christmas rope on the branches of a small tree. Only two babies were visible, skinny six-inch replicas of the mother. They were doing the "chin trick": in an effort to climb up each other, chins together, they would rise up, wobble, and fall back to the pine needles.

Marshall took off the tightly fitting screen lid and picked up a curved piece of old bark. "Under here's where the babies like to hide."

123

The lady let out a surprised squeak when she saw the pile of squirming baby snakes. "I don't believe it! There must be a hundred of them."

"Twenty-eight," Marshall said.

When the lady ran out of questions, Duncan and Marshall left the museum and headed for the Eighty-second Airborne Division tent.

Fred had no news of the hermit, so they recrossed the footbridge and went into the Lowland Woods. It was like entering a huge cathedral to come into these woods. Tall straight trunks of trees supported a high canopy of leaves that shut out the sun except for occasional openings where the light beamed in.

"Makes me mad every time I think what dumb Van Meyerding did to your soft-shell," Marshall said. "I hadn't even got to see him yet."

"He was at least as big as the snapper, Marsh."

"You know what I've been thinking, Dunc— about that judo exhibition Saturday I've been thinking maybe what Mr. Garringer says would work. A judo teacher could teach him something, and I don't mean just more judo. Like if they asked for a volunteer, who'd volunteer?"

"Van would."

"Right. And what would happen to Van if a real pro got hold of him?"

"He'd get clobbered!"

"Right," said Marshall. "So why don't we urge Mr. Garringer to be sure and tell his friend Gumpi what kind of a lesson Van needs?"

"Marshall, you're a genius. Van'll get creamed."

A narrow path led off the Nature Trail in the Lowland Woods up a steep bank to Princeton Avenue. To come down it on a bicycle you had to duck low under the branches. To go up it on foot Duncan used five handholds, a couple of small tree trunks, a large black rock, an exposed root, and a handful of grass at the top.

Duncan slid back down to the black rock. He had always wanted this rock in his collection, but it was too big to budge. "Marshall, come back here a minute. Let's see if we can move this rock. It's the one I'd like to have for the bottom of my waterfall."

The rock was smooth but pitted with small round holes, as if for millions of years water had dripped on it, hollowing out these depressions.

"It's an iceberg," Marshall said when they had tugged at it unsuccessfully for awhile. "Nine-tenths of it is buried."

"We could dig it loose," Duncan said, "but then how'd we get it home? How'd we load it in a wagon?" That was something he'd think about later.

They stopped to watch a bulldozer scooping out dirt for the basement of a house being built on Sterling Road. For Duncan's pool they would dig down about a foot, build up cement sides, and have the rock collection stuck in the cement along the top. They'd get some plastic pipe for the waterfall.

"Did you ever make anything with ready-mix cement before?" Marshall asked.

"No, but it should be easy. Just add water and mix in the wheelbarrow."

They'd build the pool and waterfall the following Saturday, they decided, but they might as well get the others together and dig up the black rock tomorrow after school. It would be easy to keep a lookout for the hermit at the same time.

When Duncan's father came home from the museum that evening all thoughts of the turtle pool flew out of Duncan's mind when he saw in his father's hand a green balloon straining up on the end of a string.

"It's for a good cause," Duncan's father said to his mother. "They're raising money for the Alan Newcomb band shell."

Duncan's leap up off the rug, where he had spread out the funnies, to ecstatically claim the balloon must have seemed strange to his parents. He felt pretty foolish when he saw them staring at him as if he'd had a relapse into early childhood. After all, the only balloons he had cared about for several years now were empty ones he could fill at the spigot for water balloon fights. He would have explained right then about the Donald Duck talk, but his mother might have some objection to his breathing helium. He'd tell them later how it all worked out.

"Thanks," he said calmly. He left the balloon resting lightly on the ceiling and went to the telephone in the hall. He closed the door and called Gates.

The Helium Balloon

"I hope you can get the knot out without busting it," Gates said. He held the green balloon while Duncan worked with teeth and fingernails first on the string and then on the knotted rubber neck of the balloon. They had gone into the Lees' garage to find out in secret the effect of the helium on their voices.

Finally the knot came loose. "Oh, no, this is scary!" Gates swayed restlessly from one foot to the other. "I wonder if it's bad for your vocal chords, like glue-sniffing can ruin your brain cells. Maybe it gives you cancer. I wonder if it tastes bad. You go first, Dunc."

"Gee, thanks. Oh, well, you gotta go sometime. Remember to grab me if I start to float up." Duncan hesitated, his heart pounding. What would it feel like? Maybe cool like the steam off of dry ice. He opened his eyes wide at Gates, put the rubber neck in his mouth, and breathed in.

To his great surprise he didn't feel anything—no tingling, no smell or taste. Maybe it wasn't going to work. He held his breath for a moment. "Does it sound funny? Quack, quack, I'm Donald Duck. Ha-ha, gosh, it works!"

Gates laughed and cracked his knuckles. "You sound crazy, Dunc. Give me a try."

Now Gates took a deep breath. With his thumbs tucked into his armpits he swaggered around the garage. "I am Jacques Cousteau, the famous deep-sea diver who invented the aqualung. . . ." At the sound of his thin falsetto voice Gates's eyes almost disappeared, and he laughed in a shrill giggle like a Disneyland beaver.

"You sound like a 33 rpm record turned up to 78," Duncan said. His voice had come back to normal. "This stuff is neat. Let's go over to the park, and try it on somebody."

It wasn't dark yet at seven o'clock, but the sky was a dull pink over the mercury vapor lights that marched along the crest of the hill by the picnic tables.

Fred was again demonstrating the folding of parachutes. When he saw Duncan and Gates, he shook his head and then went back to his memorized spiel.

"I know he won't come at night," Duncan said. "He must go to bed early."

The blue and white pontoon boat was changing musical groups under the willow tree at the Princeton Avenue "dock." The Pyromaniacs were replacing the Phantom Five. The boys were all joking around and tuning their instruments while the boat driver fiddled with the motor.

Last year at the Festival somebody cut the gas line on the boat while it was tied up overnight. Mr. Garringer said that was the "onliest" vandalism they'd had. He wondered if it might have been some musical group that hadn't been asked to play. This year any group that had ever played at a party was invited to volunteer for time on the pontoon boat.

"We could do the helium thing on *them*," Gates suggested not too eagerly.

"We could," Duncan agreed. "But let's don't." Boys that age, especially a lot of them together, didn't think much of little kid tricks. They might pop the balloon.

Farther on around the lake, past the art displays, they came to the Golden Years Club exhibit where two grandmotherly ladies sat at a counter displaying ceramic tiles and pottery. There were no visitors at the moment. "Let's spook those old ladies," Gates suggested.

"Okay, you do this one. I'll do the next."

Duncan hid behind a panelboard while Gates, with a lungful of helium, went up to the counter. A man came up beside him. Holy mackerel! It was Mr. Suber, the principal.

Gates looked up and saw him. "Hello, Gates," said Mr. Suber. Gates nodded and backed up, a pitiful smile on his face. But Mr. Suber didn't let him get away. He put his hand on Gates's shoulder and said to one of the ladies, "Mother, I want you to meet a young man in our school. This is Gates Lee. Let's see, you're in Miss MacKenzie's room this year, aren't you, Gates?"

There was a long miserable pause. Duncan's heart beat fast for poor Gates who seemed to be blowing his breath out. "No, sir," came the chipmunk voice, "I have Miss Dunlap."

Duncan cringed. Mr. Suber's eyebrows shot up, and his mouth fell open. Gates backed up and fell into a stroller with a baby in it. "Excuse me," he said to the mother, a slight distortion still in his voice.

"Just a minute, Gates," Mr. Suber said, catching hold of Gates's arm. "Do you have laryngitis? You should be home in bed with a voice like that."

Gates coughed a few times. "No, sir, I'm all right. It was a frog. I just had a frog in my throat." Gates smiled with vast relief; his normal voice had returned.

Mr. Suber hesitated. "That's funny. I thought there was something, something. . . ."

"He's a cute little scamp," Mr. Suber's mother said as Gates bolted away.

Duncan joined him behind the carving man's tent. Gates socked his forehead with the heel of his hand. "Did you see that! I'm sunk!"

Duncan began to tell the carving man, an every-year exhibitor at the Festival, what had happened, but Gates interrupted. "Let me tell it. It happened to me."

But suddenly, there was Paula! Duncan's heart bounded offbeat. She and another girl were strolling along eating purple snow cones and talking. Duncan took a gasp of helium.

"Who're you going to do it on?" Gates asked. But Duncan couldn't waste a drop of the precious helium. He'd never have had the nerve to go up to Paula and say something in his own voice, but the novelty of the trick filled him with daring.

"Hi, Paula," he said in his mousy voice. "I just saw Mr. Suber over there."

"What!" Paula actually shrieked at him. She grabbed her friend by the arm. "Duncan McKenna, what's happened to your voice? You sound creepy."

Gates came up beside Duncan, the limp balloon in his hand. In the same squeaky voice he said, "Nothing's wrong with him, he was just born that way." Then Gates folded up in shrill tinkly laughter that had all the visitors within earshot turning to stare.

"You sound like Donald Duck," Paula said. She sucked the juice off her snow cone, and she and her friend walked away.

Duncan felt crestfallen. "What a waste," he said. "She thinks we're dumb, and we're out of helium."

At a picnic table halfway up the hill to the recreation room, they found Mr. Garringer with Louie and Steve, who were eating hot dogs.

"Gimmie a bite, Louie," Duncan said. Louie offered his hot dog, holding it with his fingers close to the end, limiting the size of the bite he was willing to give away. Gates got a bite from Steve.

"Where's your guitar, Steve?" Gates asked. "They're singing over there again."

"Aw, I'm no good. I only know one song."

"You sounded pretty good over the microphone," Duncan said.

"You think so?" Steve grinned as he carefully bent his paper straw into accordion pleats. "I need to practice something new. I drew up some plans for your pool, by the way. It's got to have an overflow pipe and drainage. Let's build it Saturday."

"Not Saturday," Gates said. "We might miss, ah . . . you know who."

"Yes," Mr. Garringer said, smiling circles into his round face, "you don't want to miss my friend Gumpi Kawada."

Gates winked at Duncan. "That's right. Saturday we've got to be here."

"I mean next Saturday," Steve said.

Duncan remembered Marshall's suggestion about Van, and he asked if volunteers would get a chance to try some judo flips and holds.

"Dandy," Steve said sourly. "You know who else will be there showing off and obnoxious as usual."

This time Mr. Garringer knew who they were

talking about. "You boys better hope he's there. It's on you-all's account I arranged this. Be a step in the right direction for Van's crowd to sign up with Gumpi."

"Van's only got Conway on his side now," Steve said. "His brother's got asthma so bad they won't let him go around with Van any more, and Duffy Morton's got into the scouts for good. He got inducted into the Order of the Arrow."

Mr. Garringer nodded. "Them arrow scouts is another thing. They've got a stunt over here Saturday night, and I'm here to tell you, it'll be a humdinger. Them boys have really put out. 'Torchlight Celebration,' they call it. They don't tell me nothin' except that the main rehearsals was done out at Camp Steere. But they've been a busy bunch of boys, seein' me about every last detail, includin' they had to learn how to turn the fountain off. Now I wonder why they want the fountain off."

Duncan wondered too. A spooky Indian ceremony, no doubt. What a setting for the hermit and his dogs to plow into! "Mr. Garringer, are you on the Festival committee?"

"No, sir, I ain't. But I'm the first one to hear what they come up with."

"Well, do you know anything about an old guy with a long white beard and a bunch of Afghan dogs? My dad says . . ."

Mr. Garringer nodded. "I seen him twice. I hear they asked him to show off his dogs at a dog-training show for Sunday, but he won't have no part of anything like that, although I understand he used to show them dogs and git prizes." Mr. Garringer tapped the side of his head. "They say he's got somewhat daft from livin' all by hisself."

The Struggle on the Bank

From the steep bank of the Lowland Woods where Duncan and Gates were digging, they could hear Monroe's ancient wagon rattling down Princeton Avenue. They climbed up and looked out through the heavy foliage. Monroe was riding in the wagon; Marshall was pulling.

"They forgot shovels. I'm glad we brought the extras," Gates said.

They slid back down and continued digging around the black rock that Duncan planned to have for the base of his waterfall. "I hope Marshall remembered the rope," Duncan said. With a trench around it the rock looked twice as big as before.

Up at street level the wagon could be heard clunking up over the curb. "Gimme a push, Marsh!" And before Duncan and Gates knew what was up, here came Monroe over the crest of the bank, yelling, "Charge!" and right in his path were the two extra shovels brought from the Lees' garage.

The front wheels slammed into the two steel blades. The back wheels came up like the heels of a donkey, spilling Monroe and a coil of rope into the bushes. End over end the wagon pitched down the bank till it dropped with a shudder, wheels up and spinning, in the Nature Trail.

Monroe, with blood dripping out from under his short bangs, crawled out of the weeds. He put his arm around the trunk of a small dogwood tree and blew out his cheeks. For once the dimples were gone. "What happened?"

"You bashed into the shovels." Marshall slid down the steep grade for a closer look at Monroe's cut.

Duncan and Gates turned the wagon over. "The wagon's okay."

"It's indestructible," Monroe said. "It's made of that old-timey iron that never wears out."

"You're bleeding, Monroe," Marshall announced in his calm scientist's voice.

"Good. I hope it turns into a scar." Monroe wiped his forehead on the back of his hand and looked at the blood streak.

Gates laughed. "He wants to look tough like Van."

Marshall gave out a short, loud hee-haw. "He'll never make it with that baby face."

"I'm not always going to look like this," Monroe retorted. "I'm going to grow a beard, too."

Now Marshall really folded up laughing. "Can't

you just see Monroe eight years from now, a bearded little high school dropout with a scar on his forehead and *dimples!*"

Monroe stood up and brushed himself off. He cocked his head with a studious scowl, the dimples in deep; he seemed to be listening for a sound he couldn't quite hear. All the laughers sobered down.

"You know what?" Monroe whispered. "That spill cured my hiccoughs."

"He did have a real bad case," Marshall said.

After another quiet wait Monroe declared the hiccoughs had "evaporated. It socked 'em out of me. Come on, let's dig." He picked up a shovel and went over to inspect the rock. "Where'd it get all these holes? Bet some prehistoric gorilla stuck his foot in it when it was just soft clay by the water hole, and then a volcano spewed, and it got baked into a rock."

Marshall snorted. "Some gorilla—eight toes on one foot."

Duncan guessed that water had run over it for millions of years and dissolved out those holes. Gates said it was volcanic lava. "When it cooled, it shrank up. See, it's got ridges like a prune. Where's Steve? He'd probably know."

"At the dentist," Duncan said. "And Louie's patrolling the park. Fred's not there." He looped Marshall's rope around the rock, and everyone pulled, but the rock stayed firm. "We'll have to dig some more."

"Hope it doesn't have a big bottom," Gates said.

Monroe giggled. "Like Duffy Morton."

"Duffy's got skinnier since he went to Camp Steere," Duncan said. As they dug deeper around the rock, they speculated about what Duffy Morton and the Order of the Arrow Scouts were going to do tomorrow night by torchlight. Then they again wrapped the rope around the rock and pulled.

"It's loose! Monroe, go get the wagon." "Turn it sideways." "Lay it down!" "Straighten the wheels!" "Quick!" "Prop it up now . . ."

Instructions flew at Monroe who obligingly struggled till the wagon lay on its side touching the rock. Now, with the help of gravity, the rock could be eased over into it, and the wagon gently tipped back on its four wheels. With a little brake action from the boys, wagon and rock would then roll sedately down to the Nature Trail.

But the suction of the red clay soil didn't just gradually give up the rock. It let go all of a sudden. With the combined push-power behind it of Duncan, Marshall, and Gates, the rock lurched into the bed of the wagon, forcing it rudely back on its wheels, and rolled on out the other side. There was nothing in its way—nothing that is, except Monroe.

"Oooooof!" Monroe groaned as the rock, the size of a fat black cocker spaniel but ten times heavier, rolled across his chest, flattening him into the honeysuckle. The air came out of him with a grunt that didn't sound like Monroe. The rock thumped on down the bank to the dirt path.

The boys clustered anxiously over Monroe, who lay spread-eagled on the bank, his head considerably lower than his feet, his face turning red, the cut on his forehead bleeding again, his eyes closed.

They patted him, wiped away the blood on his forehead, and pleaded with him, "Say something, Monroe." "Are you all right?" "Where does it hurt?" "Can you hear us? Wiggle your finger if you can."

Monroe didn't wiggle his finger.

Duncan lifted his sweat shirt and looked underneath. "Oh, poor Monroe . . . but at least he's not bleeding that I can see."

Gates lightly touched Monroe's rib cage. "He could have broken ribs. That rock must weigh a ton. Oh, no!"

"He's got a pulse," Marshall said, holding Monroe's wrist. In a low monotone he said, "What I know for a fact is that children's rib bones are flexible—they may not be broken."

"Maybe he has internal injuries, like squashed lungs." Gates's brown eyes were round with worry.

Marshall shook his head. "No, Gates, or he'd be bleeding at the mouth like Steve's dog when he got hit by a car."

Duncan leaped to his feet. "I'll go get my dad. People in shock you're not supposed to move, and you should cover 'em up. Everybody take off your shirt!" Duncan peeled off his shirt and threw it to Marshall. "Cover him up."

Before Duncan could dash off to get his father,

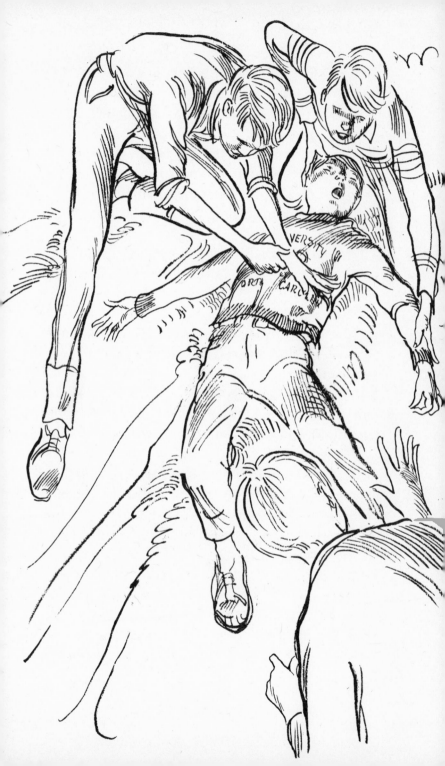

Monroe shuddered all over with a spasm that sank him a few more inches downhill.

"Convulsions," Gates whispered. "Quick, Dunc, go get your dad, Oh, poor Monroe."

Then unexpectedly Monroe began throwing off the shirts that had been tucked around him. He struggled free of the honeysuckle vines and sat up. Blood trickled down between his eyebrows. "I got 'em again," he said.

Duncan, Marshall, and Gates stared at him as if they were seeing a ghost. "What?" they all exclaimed.

"Hiccoughs. I got 'em again."

Duncan, his hands on his hips, glared at Monroe. "That was a hiccough? You were faking, Monroe."

"What?"

Marshall picked his shirt up off the ground and pulled it on over his head. "You were pulling our leg, Monroe, making us think you were out cold. It wasn't funny."

Monroe shrugged. "I must of *been* out cold." He giggled self-consciously as they all frowned at him. "Why'd you put your shirts all over me?"

"We thought you were in shock. That's why," Gates growled.

"You don't have to be mad about it. Do you wish I *was* in shock, so you could practice first aid on me?" He hiccoughed again, gasped in a deep breath, and put both hands on his chest. "That hurts."

"You'll probably be black and blue tomorrow,"

Marshall said. "In case you don't know it, you got run over by the rock."

Monroe looked down the hill at the rock. "Stupid rock. I remember, all right."

The problem now was how to load it in the wagon when there was no slope for it to roll down. They considered a pulley from an overhead tree, a ditch dug beside it to put the wagon in, and finally a teeter-totter technique by which they could lift up the rock and roll it off into the wagon.

This was the lever-and-fulcrum principle Duncan and Marshall had learned about in Science. With a long enough lever and a solid fulcrum you could lift any weight in the world. They hoped they might find a good enough lever and fulcrum at the building site on Sterling Road.

They ran up the bank and across the road and soon they had the work foreman surrounded.

He frowned, furrowing his sunburned forehead, as he listened to the problem. His eyebrows rose, and he took off his paint cap to scratch his head. "Aren't you all a tad young to be building a waterfall?" He put the paint cap back on; his curly black hair struck out under the bill.

"Heck, no," said Monroe. "It's going to have a pool too for us to get in when it's hot."

Marshall cleared his throat. "Uuuuuuuh . . . it's really for turtles, sir."

Duncan laughed. "Monroe can get in if he doesn't mind getting bitten. It'll have my rock collection around the edges too, and a drain. We've got a friend, Steve, who's going to be an engineer, and he's got some plans drawn up."

The foreman seemed to add up what he had heard and approve it. From a pile of lumber he selected what he said was a crooked piece and told the boys to help themselves to bricks. "For your fulcrum you make a double stack of bricks a little higher than the wagon," he said.

It was difficult business loading the heavy rock into the wagon by the teeter-totter method, but it worked. And once loaded, the rock sat firm as Gibraltar with the four shovels bristling around it. The wagon wheels gave out an impressive squeal as the four boys pushed and pulled it along the Nature Trail.

The Black Rock

It was late in the afternoon as Duncan, Gates, Marshall, and Monroe pushed and pulled the heavy wagon up the slope of the museum driveway. Only a few cars remained parked by the side of the road, their bumpers headed into the woods.

The Star Lady in her lavender sweater and dress came down the iron stairs from the planetarium. To Duncan the Star Lady seemed very old and wise. She had taught about the stars for so long she had begun to look like Astronomy personified. Her silver-white hair spiraled around her head like a galaxy of stars.

"Have you all seen the telescope at the Festival yet?" Duncan asked, pausing in the pull up the driveway. The Amateur Astronomers Club had set up a Questar telescope for viewing the stars at night.

"It's neat," Gates said. "You can see Saturn's rings,

145

and you can see the moon up close. It looks crumby like the Badlands of South Dakota."

"What's so bad about the Badlands?" Monroe wanted to know.

"It's like science fiction, real weirdo," Gates said.

"Nothing grows there," Duncan said, remembering a trip he had been on with his mother and father. "I caught only one horned toad when I was there. It gets so hot you could fry an egg on the hood of the car."

"Ha-ha," Monroe chirped. "What a way to mess up your car."

"I didn't say we *did* it, stupid—just that you *could*. Then at night it gets so cold you have to zip up your sleeping bag."

Marshall stopped pushing the wagon, and it rolled back a little way. "Come on, you guys. Nobody's pushing but me. Pull, Dunc."

Duncan leaned into the pulling again, and the wheels squealed. But his mind was on that Badlands trip. He turned around and pulled backwards, so he could tell about running up and down the strange formations there. "They're like huge, crusty camel's humps."

The Star Lady was catching up with them. Duncan was about to ask her if possibly the surface of the moon and the Badlands were made of the same stuff, but she spoke first, and all thoughts of the Badlands vanished from his mind. "What have you boys got there," she asked, "a meteorite?"

A *meteorite!* The wagon began to roll back. Two of the shovels knocked into Gates and fell off. He sat down on the back of it and braced with his tennis shoes. "Come on, you guys."

Nobody helped Gates hold the wagon. Duncan put his hand on the rock and stuttered, "You mean, you mean, you mean this is a meteorite?"

"Huh?" said Marshall, bereft of his usual poise around adults.

Monroe hiccoughed and beamed up at the Star Lady, his dimples in deep. "Now how about that? We'll be famous!"

The Star Lady smiled at him. She must have seen the blood and dirt smeared on his face from his two recent accidents with the wagon and the rock, but she didn't mention it. "I guess you had a difficult time digging it up," she said. "Where are you taking it?"

Duncan told her about his rock collection and the waterfall they were going to build. "Do you think it's really a meteorite?"

"I can't say for sure, but many meteorites do fall to earth and are never identified. It *could* be one."

"Uuuuuuh. What caused these indentations?" Marshall asked, his impressive low voice returned.

"Meteorites get pits like that when the weak material burns away in flight. Then you have a shooting star."

"I've seen 'em. I've seen 'em." Monroe shook his hand as if he were in school.

148

The Star Lady was so used to school kids she kept on explaining. Some meteorites were stony in composition; this looked like the metallic kind, which would be 90 per cent iron. Also it would have nickel in it and small amounts of chromium, copper, and cobalt. The true composition would have to be determined in a laboratory, but the boys could test for iron with a magnet. And they could hammer it to see if it would break. If it splintered, it wasn't an iron meteorite.

For years Duncan had admired this rock as just a rock, a handhold for climbing up the steep bank. When he had thought of it as a base for his waterfall, it had leaped in value—it became *his*. But now with every word the Star Lady spoke, he became more and more giddy.

Was it valuable? If it really was a meteorite, it was valuable, the Star Lady told them. She said that a farmer once had a meteorite for a front doorstep for years before a geologist saw it one day and guessed what it was. "We have three in our museum," she said.

"But they're nowhere near as good as this one," Monroe boasted.

The Star Lady laughed and patted Monroe on the head. "You'd better get your mother to clean up that cut." Then she got into her car and rolled down the window. "Whatever kind of rock it is, it's certainly one of the handsomest I've seen."

None of the boys had ever paid much attention to

the meteorites exhibited in the museum. Now suddenly they wanted a good look at them. They parked the wagon beside the driveway, and ran to the museum, which was just about to be locked. Miss Daisy, Duncan's father's secretary, was willing to wait. "Be quick about it though," she said. They ran around the diorama of the two fighting dinosaurs in the middle of the exhibit hall, back to the planetarium.

In the glass case were three dark, rusty, jagged rocks no bigger than baseballs—no pits, no crusty designs, no parallel flight lines. Underneath was an inscription:

> METEORITES
> *Matter from Outer Space*
> Meteorites are the remains of large meteors that have survived their 100,000 mph journey through space and their glowing fall through our atmosphere. Friction causes most meteors to burn up while rushing toward Earth; hence their popular name, shooting stars. Theories as to their origins suggest that meteors are the debris of comets or fragments resulting from the collision of small planets or asteroids.

Gates sniffed. "They're just dumb-looking rocks."
Everybody agreed. They walked past the dinosaurs—the cow-sized model of Tyrannosaurus taking a bloody bite out of the neck of the vegetarian

Triceratops—discussing how much better *their* meteorite would look in that case. Duncan could hardly wait to show his find to his father. "Thanks, Miss Daisy."

"That was quick. By the way, does that wagon belong to one of you boys? It got going downhill backward and collided with the curb."

Duncan's heart did a sickening flop when he saw the wagon upside down, and the rock, muddy bottomside up, against the curb. The driveway looped around in front of the museum entrance. The curb, encircling a plot of grass and flowers, was all that had kept the loaded wagon from crashing through the front door of the museum.

Marshall groaned. "All that work!"

Monroe kicked the rock. "Stupid meteorite."

Gates turned the wagon right side up. "At least we've still got the board and bricks. Come on, you all. Let's go get 'em."

Duncan glared at the broken curb. They'd have to fix that too. He picked up some of the crushed concrete. Dark splinters were mixed with the sandy cement. No! He looked away, frowned at the muddy bottom of the rock, his meteorite.

But he had to look back. Carefully he examined the rubble around the smashed curb. It was dirt . . . it was part of the curb. . . . But what he knew with a caved-in feeling was that those dark splinters were chips off the rock. Even a hammer couldn't chip a *real* iron meteorite, the Star Lady had said . . . but an ordinary curbstone had bashed in this rock!

Marshall, Gates, and Monroe had gone with the rattling wagon down the path to the Lowland Woods. He was glad they were gone. He wanted to mope around for a few minutes alone, to get used to the fact that the stupid meteorite had flunked its first test. It chipped. It was probably iron though. There used to be iron mines in Mecklenburg County.

Duncan's fingers fitted loosely into the rock's round pits. In the beginning this iron ore was squashed down solid by pressure and heat, and then for millions of years it just sat and weathered. Maybe a stream flowed over it, and grains of sand swirled around in whirlpools to gouge out these little smooth holes.

By the time he heard the squeal of the wagon coming back down the trail loaded with bricks, Duncan had reasoned himself out of his initial disappointment that the rock was only a rock.

"It's about time you showed up," Marshall complained. "What were you doing, talking to your famous meteorite?"

"You want to know something? That famous meteorite got bashed in by the curb. It's not one. But I'm glad. If it were real, we'd have to give it up to the museum, and we need it for the waterfall."

With the rope they dragged the rock up on the end of the long board. They stacked up bricks under it, for the fulcrum, and sat on the other end of the lever. Up came the rock. It was easy to slide it off into the wagon.

"Louie didn't come," Gates remarked. "No hermit."

Actually no one had expected him. It was to-morrow, Saturday, that they all hoped would be the day for the hermit's annual appearance at the Festival.

"But," Marshall added with a sinister chuckle, "I hope not till after we've seen Van get smeared at his own game."

A Load of Free Cement

The giant lopsided body of the Concrete Supply truck wasn't revolving as it lumbered away from the curb in front of the house being built on Sterling Road. On the ground was a squashy glob—enough to fill a bathtub—of the wet mixture left from the day's work.

"I see you got your rock okay," the foreman said. He helped Duncan and Marshall unload the bricks that had been stacked behind the rock in the wagon. Monroe and Gates carried the crooked piece of lumber back to the lumber pile.

"We got your board awful dirty," Monroe said.

"Not half as dirty as you got yourselves. It's a good-looking rock for your waterfall."

"It's a meteorite," said Monroe.

"Monroe, you know doggone well it isn't. It chipped," Marshall said.

Monroe shrugged a few times and grinned, "Oh, well, it's more fun that way."

Duncan nudged the toe of his shoe into the mushy mixture dumped by the Concrete Supply truck. "That's a lot of good cement."

The foreman said it was concrete. "It has gravel in it. Cement is when it's mixed with sand for brick-work."

"Is it not any good anymore?"

"Sure it's good. It's just left over. You want it?"

"Gosh . . . I don't know. We weren't planning to build yet . . . but I suppose we *could*."

"Yeh, sure, Dunc," Gates laughed. "It'll be hard by morning."

"Why couldn't we use it now?"

Marshall cleared his throat. "Uuuuuuuuh, that's not practical, Duncan."

"Why not?"

Marshall had a lot of reasons. It would soon be dark. They didn't have the plastic pipe yet. Steve would be mad if they did it without his plans when he'd already drawn them up, and everybody's mother would be mad because it was time to eat. Duncan had answers for all of Marshall's objections, and the more he jiggled with his foot this puddle of really professionally made concrete, the more he wanted it.

"Come to think of it, Marshall," Monroe piped up, "You're the one that's not practical. This stuff is *free*."

155

"How long before it gets stiff?" Gates asked.

"Keep it turned, and it'll last you long enough," the foreman said. "Do you want it, or don't you?"

They did. The foreman brought a trowel and a large wheelbarrow from the toolshed. "I'll lend you these till tomorrow," he said.

With the four shovels they quickly filled the wheelbarrow with the soft concrete, making a load that was much too big for the boys to handle. "I'll man the wheelbarrow," the foreman said.

Monroe protested politely that they really didn't want to be any bother, that the foreman was a real busy man and all that. Then he giggled and shrugged his long sweat shirt up and down. The man laughed. "No trouble at all," he said. He picked up the handles. "Head out."

The smoothest route home was back to Princeton and up Maryland Avenue. Marshall and Monroe led the way with the rattling wagon containing the four shovels and the black rock.

At the McKenna's steep driveway Duncan and Gates helped push first the wagon and then the wheelbarrow. "Thanks," the foreman said. "Dadgum stuff gets heavy." He set it down in the McKenna's backyard and told Monroe to "keep her turned." He examined the rocks in Duncan's collection behind the gardenia bush and looked the place over, as if planning the job.

Duncan went in to call Steve and Louie on the phone. His mother asked who was the man out there. "He gave us some free concrete," Duncan said.

"What in the world for?" she asked. "Dinner's nearly ready."

Almost before Duncan hung up the phone, Louie dashed in the back door with a drumstick in his hand. "Hi, Mrs. McKenna." He waved the drumstick and brought two biscuits out of his shirt pocket. "They're all buttered and jammed."

"Louie, you're a mess," Duncan's mother said, smiling. "Now, Duncan, what about this cement?"

"It's concrete, Mom. The brick-laying stuff's cement. This stuff's mixed with gravel."

"Duncan, what about it?"

Steve came in the front door, calling for Duncan. He had a clipboard with three pages of figuring he had worked up for the project. "I'll be out in a minute, Steve. Go show your plans to the man in the backyard."

Steve went out letting the door slam.

Duncan's father came into the kitchen. "What's going on around here?"

"We're going to build the pool, Dad."

"Hold on a minute, Duncan. What pool? You might let me in on your plans."

"I did, Dad. Remember? You liked the idea. It's for turtles."

"I remember, Dave," Duncan's mother said. "It's to be a memorial for that big turtle that drowned in Duncan's book satchel."

"Drowned in what?" What Mrs. McKenna meant finally dawned on him. "Oh, yes, I remember. The lake. I'll be glad when the Festival's over. I've got a million things on my mind. But what's the commotion out there, Duncan? Who's that man?"

"I don't know his name, Dad. He's the man who gave us the stuff."

"What stuff?"

"The concrete."

They went out to the backyard, and the foreman introduced himself. "My name's Bert Davis. We're building over there on Sterling." Duncan's father shook hands with Bert, but he didn't look too pleased to see him and his full wheelbarrow. "Maybe I put my foot in it," Bert said. "If this job's just something the kids dreamed up . . ." He began to pick up the wheelbarrow.

"No, no, not at all. It was good of you. But frankly, Duncan"—he turned a bushy frown on Duncan—"I didn't know this pool was going to be so elaborate. I thought what you had in mind was a natural pool with a dirt bottom and sand."

"But this'll be better, Dad. The other kind would get gunky and be hard to keep clean."

"But still, right here at dinnertime, Duncan. . . ."

"But the stuff is free, Dad. We won't have to buy ready-mix cement."

Bert picked up the wheelbarrow handles. "I'm sorry. I should have kept my big mouth shut. I'll dump it at the curb and hose it down."

"No, now, don't do that," Duncan's father said, glancing at the glum faces of Marshall, Monroe, and Gates who leaned on shovels, listening to the conversation. "Put it down, Bert. Leave it. I'm outnumbered. Actually it was very good of you to take an interest. Thanks so much. We'll get on with it right now. Dinner can wait." He shook hands with Bert again. "We've held you up now long enough. Thanks again. Thanks very much."

But Bert didn't want to leave. "I'll help you get the job off the ground," he said. "I've built one of these before."

He told how years ago he and his army buddies in New Guinea had built a pool for hot showers. A gasoline pump raised the river water up the hill to the pool, the sun heated the water, and the drain was finished in a faucet with a shower head.

"This sort of takes me back," he said. "Show me those plans again, Steve. Some of you boys begin to dig out the foundation. Steve, show them where. And lay out the inflow and drainage lines. Dig the trenches narrow so as not to mess up too much grass. Save the sod. Duncan, lay out your rocks as you want them for the edge of the pool and the waterfall. You"—he pointed to Monroe—"keep on turning."

"Right, chief!" Monroe flew into a stiff salute and speeded up the troweling of the concrete.

Duncan's father volunteered to go and get the pipe and fittings, but Bert said he'd do it. He knew a place that stayed open till nine, and also he'd bring a leveler from his car. He looked again at Steve's plans. "Thirty-two feet of inch-and-a-quarter pipe, eighteen feet of half-inch."

Duncan's mother came to the window and said that anyone whose mother didn't know where he was had better come in and telephone home.

Marshall went in, but Monroe said, "Not me! She'd tell me to come home."

"I'll call her for you," Duncan's mother said.

When Bert returned with the pipe over his arm, the trenches and the pool's foundation had been dug. The pool would be oblong. In the shallow water under the waterfall the baby soft-shells could indulge their favorite pastime, hiding under the sand with only their sneaky black eyes showing. Occasionally, like periscopes from small submarines, their pointed snouts would rise to the surface for a breath of air and a look around.

Bert attached a threaded coupling to the upper end of the drainage pipe, and into it he screwed an eighteen-inch length of metal pipe. "Now, for the overflow here, we have to figure a way to support this pipe up vertical till the concrete hardens down here around the coupling."

An eight-foot tomato stake nailed to Tony's tree would serve that purpose. As Bert pounded the nail in the tomato stake, a stubby pencil dropped down from overhead. "Well, I'll be darned," Bert said as he looked up into the black masquerade face that

161

peered over the edge of Tony's platform in the pine tree.

"That's Tony. He likes pencils."

"He'll like your baby turtles, too," Bert said.

"He won't get the chance. We'll take him out to the lake and let him go pretty soon."

"Okay, men, we'll pour now. Just as we did it in New Guinea."

As Bert sang "Waltzing Matilda," the concrete was dumped and spread around. All hands were in it. The rocks along the edges were overhung slightly so the turtles wouldn't be able to climb out. Then the black rock was hosed off and dragged into position. The inflow pipe was laid in the ground and bent up over the black rock. Around it were piled and cemented in place the rocks Duncan had picked to form the mountain.

At the top was Duncan's most highly prized rock specimen, a broken geode. It was the size of a cantaloupe with pink crystals inside. Now at the top of the rock pile it was a miniature cave with pink stalactites. Out of the mouth of the geode cave would gush a stream of water.

"Give it a light sprinkle before you go to bed and again in the morning," Bert said, "but don't turn on the fountain or disturb any of these rocks till it's set a couple of days."

Bert left with the wheelbarrow then. Duncan's friends had already gone. The backyard spotlight was on, catching the sparkle of mica on some of the rocks. Over at the park the evening Festival program had begun; faint music drifted in on the still night air. Duncan ran up the steps to supper, famished.

"These hamburgers are sure to be as tough as shoe leather," Duncan's mother said as he sat down at the table. "They were done two hours ago."

Duncan bit through the stiff bun into a hamburger that—yes, it was *that tough*. But if supper had been eaten when it was first ready, the pool wouldn't have been built. "They're good," he said, grinning around a mouthful.

"What a politician," his father laughed. "Come on, Duncan, admit it. It's tough as a boot. It's the price you pay for that free concrete."

Duncan reconsidered the hamburger. "It's like I've got a mouthful of pencil erasers with ketchup."

"What a way to talk about the food," his mother said. "Even if it's true. Mrs. Jordan called you, by the way. She wants her yard cut and trimmed, the gutters cleaned, and the driveway and garage swept."

"Maybe she'd like her car washed, too," Duncan said.

"Duncan, are you being sarcastic? If you don't want the job, just say so. I didn't commit you. I said I'd have you call her when you got your hands out of the cement."

"No, I *do* want the job," Duncan mumbled through a mouthful of cottage cheese and lettuce.

He realized he was hard for his mother to figure out. (He hadn't yet explained what he and Gates had done with the helium balloon.) Never before had he been glad of a request for yardwork, but now he wanted all he could get. There was a possibility that the hermit might never come to the Festival. So the sooner he started making some yardwork money, the better. "I can start the job in the morning, but I've got to be over at the park in the afternoon. Van Meyerding's going to get creamed!"

He told his parents about the judo exhibition and how he and his friends all hoped it would turn out to be Van's Waterloo. Then at night there would be the mysterious Order of the Arrow thing by torchlight. But the major unknown for Saturday, he kept to himself. And as he sprinkled the concrete pool after supper and later as he lay in bed with Tony purring beside him, he thought about it. Tomorrow could be the day that the wild-eyed hermit would come.

Duncan closed his eyes and thought of the giant bearded man striding in army boots beside the lake, led on by a team of five feathered hounds the color of sand, pacing in rhythm like Lippizaner steeds. It was a long time before he went to sleep.

The Judo Lesson

When Duncan and Gates arrived at the amphitheater Saturday afternoon at two o'clock, the
schedule was running twenty minutes late. Fred
was at his post with the parachute, but they didn't
need to ask him about the hermit. They already
knew he hadn't come. Gates had spent the morning
on the lookout, and Louie, Steve, and Marshall were
here now, waiting for them on the green benches.
The Memorial Hospital nurses' choir was singing.

Concerts were usually held on the island, with the
clipped bushes for wings and backdrop, but for the
Festival the island stage had become the Coffeepot
Café. Only teen-agers over fifteen were allowed on
the island. So the Festival events were held directly
in front of the amphitheater seats on a prefabricated
stage.

A moving van was parked behind the stage, its
back doors slightly ajar. Duncan and Gates peeked

in. "Canoes!" Duncan whispered. "For the Order of the Arrow thing, I bet."

"I bet they're going to land 'em on the island," Gates said. "That's why they had to find out how to turn the fountain off."

The nurses were singing about Oklahoma, "where the corn is as high as an elephant's eye," when Gates and Duncan found Marshall, Louie, and Steve in the front row of the audience.

Marshall leaned across Louie and Steve. "Hey, Dunc, I asked Mr. Garringer about getting Van for a volunteer, and he's going to do it."

"But he's not here," Steve said, looking at his watch. "It'd be just like him not to show up the one time we want him to."

There was much clapping, and the nurses filed off the stage.

The appearance of Gumpi Kawada was no surprise to Duncan. He knew from Mr. Garringer that Gumpi was a little Japanese man about Steve's size, which was hardly bigger than Duncan. The surprise was one of Gumpi's advanced students. She was a girl! And Duncan knew he had seen her somewhere before. She was delicate like Gumpi, and she was dressed like him in a loose pajama costume. Her head tipped a little forward, so that her straight brown hair fell partly over one eye and curved around to her chin. Where had he seen her before? As he stared at her, he could see her behind a desk with a microphone hanging down. Yes! She was the drive-in bank teller. Miss Mavis Anthony was her name.

Duncan passed on this information to his friends. "She looks like she's thirteen," Louie said, and added that when he grew up he was going to put his money in that bank.

"She'll be gone by then," Steve laughed, his black-rimmed glasses slipping halfway down his nose. He checked his watch again. "Monroe isn't here either."

The exhibition began with Miss Mavis Anthony strolling along the stage, her pocketbook under her arm, looking through make-believe store windows. A big hunk of a man slunk along behind her. He made a grab for her pocketbook. But before he could get it, Miss Mavis let out a spine-tingling scream, spun the man around, ducked his fist, jerked him, tripping him over her foot, until he sprawled headfirst and the purse slid across the stage.

Offstage a whistle blew, and a policeman dashed in. When he saw Mavis, holding an armlock on the man, he scratched his head, pushing his cap back, and said through the microphone that hung from a cord around his neck, "Lady, you don't seem to *need* any help."

Everybody laughed, and Mavis let go of the purse snatcher. Then Gumpi made a short speech about judo, which he called the gentle art. Louie whispered, "I've changed my mind about that girl. She's too gentle." Judo is an ancient and honorable sport in Japan, Gumpi said, like wrestling, archery, and fencing. A more aggressive Oriental contest is karate, which can kill an opponent. Learning judo and karate, Gumpi said, requires rigorous mental and physical discipline. Hundreds of techniques must be learned for putting an opponent off balance, so that he can then be tripped, thrown, choked, or held powerless. "Miss Anthony has just demonstrated the use of several judo techniques in outwitting an opponent twice her weight."

Duncan whispered to Steve, "Boy, would I ever love to see her do that to Van Meyerding!"

The exhibition continued with members of Gumpi's youngest classes happily tumbling each other around the mats.

Monroe finally arrived, panting as if he'd run all the way. He had a Band-Aid on his forehead. He plopped down on his knees in the grass in front of Duncan. "Van's down there listening to the pontoon boat," he said.

"He ought to be here watching judo," Gates said.

"He thinks he knows it all," Steve grumbled. "Since Mr. Garringer wants him to come, that's probably what he won't do even if it kills him."

Monroe giggled. "Hope it does. Let him rot."

But Louie with his finger pointing up said, "No, Monroe. Better he should tangle with this little cutie-pie we just saw and die of embarrassment when she flips him."

Gumpi with a microphone around his neck,

walked cat-footed around the stage. He watched every movement of his students, often spoke to them in whispers, and then in his melodious voice would tell the audience the uses of each technique.

The exhibition was over, and still there was no sign of Van.

Mr. Garringer towered above Gumpi and Mavis. He beckoned to Duncan. "You boys come over here. This here's my friend Gumpi Kawada, and I want you to meet Miss Mavis Anthony."

Monroe shrugged his shoulders and dimpled up at Mavis. "I know it. We saw her."

"But you missed the best part, Monroe, when she flipped the guy trying to get her pocketbook."

Gumpi asked Duncan why he was interested in judo, but before Duncan could answer, how he'd sure like to learn to defend himself, Mr. Garringer put his big freckled hand on Gumpi's shoulder and said "Yonder comes the boy I told you about."

It didn't take long to spot Van. In a dark-red shirt and white pants he loped along the edge of the lake.

Duncan, on the grass by the wrestling mat watched uneasily as Van sauntered up to be introduced to Gumpi. Van still wore on his knuckle a Band-Aid to cover the stitches where Big Neck had bitten him. Gumpi just might be the one to wipe the smirk off that arrogant face. With his mysterious smile, folded hands, and tiny feet, he could be one of those Oriental holy men who can walk over hot coals without getting burned. He might have special powers over people. He had certainly hypnotized Mr. Garringer about the virtues of judo.

"Want you to meet Van Meyerding," Mr. Garringer said to Gumpi. "He's the one I told you was all fired up about judo."

With a lopsided smile on his face, Van looked Gumpi up and down, thinking, Duncan supposed, that it would be fun to give this little shrimp a flip.

"I understand that you've been studying a book of judo," Gumpi said, bowing slightly. His folded hands rested lightly over his black belt, which was tied in a knot at his waist.

Van brought out a curly-paged book from his back pocket and showed it to Gumpi. He read the title aloud: "*Judo Made Easy* by Burlinghouse. I've especially studied the diagrams. I think I understand it pretty good. I just need somebody regular to practice on."

Gumpi, whose head was on a level with Van's shirt pocket, nodded and smiled, his hands still primly folded over his black belt. "Yes, practice is essential. You may become a fine beginner."

Oh, oh! Duncan nudged Steve. Van wasn't going to like that. Sure enough, he didn't. He rocked up on his toes and dropped back on his heels, his hands on his hips.

"Well, I wouldn't say I was just a beginner," he drawled.

"We'll see." Gumpi nodded pleasantly.

Mr. Garringer interrupted then. A good crowd of children had gathered and were impatiently waiting for things to begin. "All right, boys and girls." Mr. Garringer raised his hand for attention. "I want you all to meet my friend Gumpi Kawada."

Gumpi went to the center of the mat; with his palms placed together, he bowed from the waist in such a solemn way that immediate silence settled over the rowdy children. Mr. Garringer settled himself on a picnic bench and loosened his shoelaces as Gumpi explained the meaning of the bow he had just made. "Classes begin with this courteous address between opponents." Duncan glanced at Van, sitting cross-legged across the mat from him. His face was set in a smirk.

Gumpi then said he'd ask one of his advanced students to demonstrate the teaching of a few simple techniques, and he'd need a volunteer.

Van's hand shot up, then dropped to his lap. "I'd do it, but you might want a victim that doesn't know anything about judo."

"Yes," Gumpi said, smiling his round smile. "I want someone totally unskilled. You will be fine."

Duncan and Steve knocked elbows. Monroe pinched Duncan's leg. Duncan clapped his chin into his hand to hold down the grin that wanted to pop out all over his face. Didn't Gumpi know what an insult that was to Van? He had as much as told him he didn't know beans about judo.

Van rose slowly off the mat, his face set in a scowl. "Don't you think I know anything about judo? I've been studying it for two years. If you want someone totally unskilled, you'd better get someone else."

Gumpi, his face still wreathed in the moon smile, turned his neatly manicured hands up like an open book. "From a book you have studied."

"Yesssss," Van hissed. Then he whirled halfway around. He pointed across the mat at Duncan. "He can tell you how good I am."

Duncan jerked as if a bee had stung him and nodded yes, remembering the many times Van had tangled his feet up and dumped him.

Gumpi stroked his chin, nodding. "It would be well to have someone of your build, strong and agile. But if your reflexes in judo are well established you are right. It would not illustrate the point I want to make, that no matter how well coordinated and strong a person is, he is helpless against the techniques of a person much smaller but skilled in judo. Ah, well. . . ." He came out of his contemplation with a smile and a hand outstretched to Van. "What say we give it a try, my friend? Mavis, please come and demonstrate how you would resist a frontal attack."

Mavis, who had been almost out of sight behind the children, hopped up, pulling her tunic down smooth under the heavy brown belt that was wrapped twice around her small waist. She bowed to Van.

173

Van's mouth fell halfway open at the sight of Mavis. He was apparently seeing her for the first time. "A girl? I don't want to hurt a girl."

"She can take care of herself," Gumpi said. "I want you to attempt to throw her down. Take hold of the lapel and sleeve of her tunic as I am sure it is depicted in the book."

"I know, I know." Van reached out and seized Mavis by the left sleeve and the right lapel.

Duncan's heart was thumping away with a mixture of hope and fear. Maybe Mavis knew more judo, but Van wouldn't be a pushover. He was full of tricks. Mavis's shining hair fell over one eye in a curve toward her smiling mouth. Her hands hung loose from the big sleeves of her costume as Van rigidly faced her.

Duncan chewed his knuckle. Be careful, Mavis! But Van couldn't endure her straightforward eyes. He dropped his attention to the mat and let go of her tunic. "I can't do it to a girl," he said.

Gumpi's hand went up. "All right, another volunteer?"

"No, no. I'll do it!" Van ground his fist into the palm of his other hand. He took the position again and frowned down into Mavis's pert smile. Then, as if not allowing himself another moment's shattering delay, he jerked her lapel and spun around in front of her, as he had done several times to Duncan with disastrous results for Duncan. But this time something astonishing happened. Van's white tennis

174

shoes sailed through the air over Mavis's back, and before Van could whack down on the mat, she caught him, dangled him by one leg and one arm. Then gently she set him down.

"The first thing we teach our students is to fall correctly," Gumpi said, speaking rapidly. "You will notice that our student didn't let the volunteer take the fall lest he be injured."

Duncan, Louie, Steve, Monroe, Gates, and Marshall were all bunched together, punching each other and trying to stifle their giggles.

Van leaped up red-faced. His hands raked his disheveled hair. "I know how to take a fall," he growled.

Gumpi shook his head. "Don't risk it, Mavis."

Van glared at him. "I wasn't ready. How was I to know a girl would be so rough. Now I know how she plays, I'll know what to do."

"Go through it slowly, Mavis. Show him how it was done."

But Van didn't want to be shown. He took Mavis roughly by the sleeve and lapel, pulled quickly, spun his hip around, and the same thing happened. His feet sailed in an arc as he rolled over Mavis's shoulders. Her hair swung back as she broke his fall just short of the ground. She looked as combed and composed as she did when she said, "Good afternoon," in the drive-in teller window at the bank.

But Van was in a daze. He got to his feet, panting and staring at Mavis with a mixture of frustration and rage that worried Duncan. When Van got mad, look out. Look what happened to Big Neck!

Mavis was too good and gentle to understand this. "Come into it slowly, and I'll teach you," she said softly.

This time Van was determined. He moved even more savagely and tried a different trick. His foot lunged out as if he hoped to hook his heel around Mavis's leg. But it didn't work. She had a little kick of her own that had Van so off-balance that he let out a grunt, lurched in a disorganized sprawl, and ended up cradled like a baby in Mavis's lap.

Duncan let out a yelp of glee as he had when Van got hobbled by the parachute ropes. All around the mat fun broke out. The children squealed and wrestled on the grass and plied each other with their amateur judo chops, armlocks and leg holds.

Van wasn't aware of any of this. He paced back and forth in front of Mavis like a nervous cheetah. "Would you like to go through it slowly so you can understand your mistakes?" she asked sweetly.

"Yesssss!" he snarled.

After another unsuccessful try to upset Mavis, Van stayed on his knees on the mat. As he looked up into Mavis's smiling eyes, something surfaced in Van's face that erased the rage from his expression. His shoulders sagged, and he breathed through his mouth. He stared at her as if he had never seen anything like her before.

Duncan stopped grinning. The horseplay on the

grass stopped. Suddenly it was quiet. Into Duncan's mind flashed a memory. Someone slipped on a rock in Sugar Creek and fell in, and everyone laughed. But when he just lay there and blood made a streak in the water from his head, the laughing stopped, and the boy who was hurt was helped to shore.

"Thank you, Mavis." Gumpi bowed slightly. Mavis bowed back and retreated. Van stood up. The full sleeves of Gumpi's costume hung down from his folded arms in peaks, giving him an appearance of imperial Oriental majesty. "No one can excel in judo by just studying a book, Van." Gumpi's voice had a soft liquid rhythm. "You must learn to feel every move of an opponent before he makes it. This you can't learn from a book. Do you understand?"

Van nodded as if from deep inside a trance.

"Yes. As the blind develop an awareness of their surroundings, we learn to sense an opponent's next move and to counter it with an instantaneous reflex. It takes years to learn this." Gumpi's small hands were pressed together in a praying position. "Judo is called the gentle art because it makes an art of yielding. At the right moment we yield, to surprise and gain advantage over our assailant. Judo is a sport to be enjoyed; it is also useful in the defense of ourselves and others. It is never used aggressively. As the gentle art is learned we acquire self-confidence, self-discipline, and keen judgment."

Small cold bumps lifted the hairs on Duncan's arms as he listened to Gumpi talking to Van. His words rippled like water over rocks. Van never shifted his eyes from Gumpi's face. His hands pressed against the long red shirttail that hung over his white jeans. "One must learn humility, Van, to compete in this sport where even a young girl can be your master. You will be a quick student because you care very much. You are the kind of student I look for. Come here, Van. . . ."

Van was a puppet in Gumpi's hands. He let himself be pushed, turned, bent, and jerked by the wrist, shirt, and belt as Gumpi talked about center of balance and how to use the knowledge of it.

Anything Gumpi told Van to do, Van did. And he nodded yes, he would like to learn a new vocabulary of Japanese judo terms. Gumpi bowed to Van, and Van bowed back. "Will you come to the *dojo* on Saturday?"

"What time?"

"Ten o'clock."

For another moment or two, Van stood there in a daze, seemingly unaware that around the mat in a silent circle were about three dozen children who thought they knew Van Meyerding and could hardly believe what they saw. Then he turned and sped off under the trees to the path along the crest of the hill.

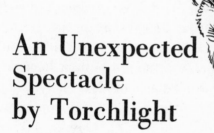

An Unexpected
Spectacle
by Torchlight

It was the overwhelming smell of overripe dead fish that woke Duncan up. He might have slept on and on through the Order of the Arrow event at the Festival were it not for that powerful stench, which was part of a bad dream in which he was caught and hugged to the chest of some bearlike beast. He thrashed his head from side to side, jolting himself awake and upsetting Tony whose leathery, fishy-smelling hands had been mashing his nose.

"Beat it, Tony, you masher!" Duncan sat up, spitting out raccoon hairs and wiping his mouth with the back of his hand.

He wasn't in bed, he discovered. He was behind the gardenia bush where his rock collection used to be. Apparently he had fallen asleep here after supper when he came out to admire his new turtle pool. Actually he was worn to a frazzle. That's why he had sprawled out on the ground, his feet on Tony's tree.

Except for one thing, it had been a great day. The one thing he had kept hoping all afternoon would happen hadn't happened. The hermit hadn't come. But Duncan had made four dollars doing yardwork that morning, which was a good start toward getting rid of his debt to Louie. Never again would he put money in a shirt pocket without a button. Recovering the lost money seemed less and less likely as the week ran out of time. The hermit would probably not come at all.

Duncan relaxed against the tree. There was only one thing left over at the Festival that he really wanted to do. He wanted to master the trick of the rope bridge. After the judo show he had kept his eye on the bridge for a time when the line would be short. He had walked around the lake again, looking at everything and still the line was too long.

The music from the park two blocks away had stopped. He sat up, listening for it to begin again. But now the lights over there were beginning to dim. He leaped off the ground and raced up the back steps, yelling, "Hey, Mom, what time is it?"

"Don't yell so, Duncan. I can hear you."

"What time is it?"

His mother looked at her wristwatch. "Nine o'clock."

"Whew! I might have missed it." He let the door slam.

"Missed what?"

"The Arrow thing."

The clouds in the sky over the park reflected a faint glow from the city, but the Festival, except for the usual mercury vapor lights and the lanterns of the Coffeepot Café on the island, looked oddly dim. The tent lights were off, and so was the fountain.

In the eerie illumination, the people and their clothes were all black, white, and gray. Trailing black willow wands swayed over the sparkling lake. Something was about to happen. Duncan could feel it in his pounding pulse as he ran across the Princeton Avenue bridge.

The next moment it began. Three yellow flares lit up the trailing willow branches, turning them green again. And then into the lighted circles strode three Indian chiefs with bristling costumes and painted faces. By the time Duncan had slipped his way up to the front of the crowd, three aluminum canoes had been lifted aloft by six bare-chested braves.

The yellow torches, sunk on their long spear shafts in the muddy beach, lit up the embarkation with a flickering radiance. It was heart of pine wood they used for the torches, Duncan assumed. Nothing else he could think of would flare up and burn so steadily.

As the canoes were set in the water, the three

resplendent chiefs waited with folded arms and scowling faces. One of them wore buffalo horns on his head and a prickly necklace of bones. He was the medicine man, no doubt, with sunken eyes and spotted face—a face to spook away evil spirits. From the back of his magnificent buffalo horns fell a train of multicolored feathers reaching to his moccasined heels.

The three chiefs stood like statues of real Indians Duncan had seen at the Smithsonian Institution in Washington, D.C. The only motion Duncan could see was the slight shifting of the fingers of the medicine man as his hand cupped around his elbow.

Something about that hand caught Duncan's attention and held it. Somewhere before he had seen those restless fingers. Square stubby fingers . . . with clean, closely bitten, almost no fingernails. . . . Of course! Duffy Morton. It was Duffy, who used to be in Van's gang.

The motionless chiefs came to life when the torches had been fastened to the bows of the canoes. Keeping his moccasins dry, Duffy stepped into a canoe, careful to steady his buffalo horns. So mindful was he of the balance of the horns that he didn't notice that the end of his train of feathers had fallen overboard. At least two feet of it floated on the surface of the water as he settled himself in the center of the canoe.

The people who saw it whispered and pointed, but Duffy didn't seem aware of what had happened. The brave in the stern of the canoe calmly fished it out with his paddle and laid it over a thwart to drip.

Like the children of Hamelin led by the Pied Piper, the crowd followed the canoes along the edge of the lake. They separated and streamed around the panelboards and tents, wondering what would happen next. The sound of their wondering was a low hum.

Counterclockwise the canoes rounded the curve of the lake, laying behind a silvery train. Occasional sparks dropped from the torches and hissed when they hit the lake. With the fountain off an unnatural hush pervaded the moonlit scene. Teenagers at the exclusive Coffeepot Café left their tables and swarmed to the end of the island to watch this procession of early Americans.

But presently as the canoes neared the island, the solemn mood was blasted to bits as the six braves pivoted the canoes around and let out shrill whoops. They churned up the water in quick chopping strokes, the start of a mad race down the lake. Under the trailing boughs of the willow tree they turned around and came back in formation, paddling to the rhythm of a chant.

The canoes were beached on the shore of the island, displacing a flock of disgruntled ducks. Now it was apparent why the fountain had been turned off. The torches and Indians would have been doused by the spray. The teen-agers whooped it up as the braves and their sputtering torches, followed by the chiefs, filed past the dark clipped hedges onto the lantern-lighted stage of the Coffeepot Café, weaving between the tables with their red-and-white checkered cloths and dripping candles.

Duncan, who had run around the lake to the shore of the narrow channel by the rope bridge, had a good view of all this. The Indians trooped over the wooden bridge to the mainland where they were followed by a swelling crowd up the hill, past the first-aid station, through a picnic shelter, and down the hill to stop finally just beyond the Freedom Park Special, an old retired steam locomotive on the edge of the baseball field.

Here a tepee had been set up. Cross-legged in front of it, a tom-tom beater, decorated with paint and dressed in a breechclout and two rabbit-ear feathers, was so engrossed in his drumming that he seemed not to know that a large crowd had gathered. He never looked up even as the chiefs and the six paddlers with their lighted torches formed a half circle around him.

Then the rhythm changed. People swayed back out of the way as six more Indians fluttered out of the tepee with wings attached to their arms. Like eagles soaring, they whirled; their wings banked and tilted, making a breeze in the faces of the watchers. It was a marvel to Duncan that with the six of them weaving around in a small space, there were no collisions. Duffy and the two chiefs solemnly approved the dance. Their faces gleamed with sweat as they stood with folded arms, their backs to the tepee in their long-sleeved heavily beaded jackets and fringed leggings.

When the dancers had flown inside the tepee and closed the flap, Duncan looked around the crowd. Gates was across the circle staring with a big beaver-toothed grin at the medicine man. He must have guessed it was Duffy. And Paula! Duncan's heart as usual turned over at the sight of her. Her hair was in braids tied with yellow ribbons. She had in her hands, as if she were handling a baby Easter chick, a fluffy pink-and-blue armband that had dropped off one of the dancers.

Duncan shifted his gaze to the old locomotive behind Paula. Children were perched all over it like birds on a barn roof. Louie was up front on the bell. On the baseball field at second base, Duncan could see Steve with his guitar and Marshall. A bonfire had been built there, presumably by the Order of the Arrow scouts, and neat white puffs of smoke—signals, no doubt—were rising in the still air to disappear in the dark above the lighted ballfield.

Now the tom-tom began again with a fiercer, faster beat. Out of the tepee, like football players from the locker room, pranced the six braves dressed in horsehair headdresses, paint, and breechclouts.

Halfway through the dance, a good idea popped into Duncan's mind. If he was ever going to find the rope bridge unoccupied, now would be the time when all the kids were here watching the Indians. He got up, and stepping around and over the children on the grass, headed back toward the bridge.

The lights were all on again, but the fountain was still off. Music was coming from the stage where the Charlotte Symphony was playing something vigorous. And he was right: no one was on the bridge. He bought a package of peanut-butter crackers at the snack truck and something he'd never tried before, an imitation black raspberry smash.

At the platform he took his time planning a careful strategy. He had heard that by taking big slow steps you could have a reasonably smooth trip. He decided to try big *fast* steps, to run so fast that the bounce wouldn't catch up with him till he was already at the island platform.

He squashed the empty paper cup, and put it and the cellophane from the crackers in his pocket. He had gone only four leaps when he realized that the plan was an absolute dud. A heaving was set up like nothing he had ever before experienced. By the time he was midway to the island, a grisly sensation hit him right where the imitation black raspberry smash was.

Clinging to the rope railings, he tried to quiet the thrashing of the bridge, but nothing helped the feeling inside. He finally made it to the high platform at the island. Too weak to stand up, he sank to the wooden planks and lay there gasping for breath, fearful that at any moment the dreadful nausea would force him into an embarrassing situation. He longed to climb down and lie on the cool grass, to wait for the misery to go away. But there was that sign, written in Magic Marker on poster paper, tacked to a tree trunk:

PRIVATE PROPERTY

TRESPASSERS WILL BE MUGGED

SIGNED THE COFFEEPOT COMMITTEE

He didn't dare challenge that sign. Teen-agers were everywhere, sprawled in groups and in couples on the grass. He put his head on his arm, closed his eyes, and breathed deeply.

It seemed a long time that he lay there with his head whirling and his stomach in an uproar. Finally the crisis passed. He yawned and propped himself up on his elbows.

The Indians were returning. He watched them cross the bridge to the island. From the Coffeepot there came the howl of "Redskins!" Some teen-agers dove under the red-and-white tablecloths.

Duncan turned around now so he could watch the embarkation. The torches were fastened to the foreward thwarts. Three braves held the bows while the three important personages settled themselves in the middle positions.

Duffy was in the last canoe. Duncan grinned as the same thing that happened before happened again. Duffy's train of feathers fell in the water. But this time the stern paddler was busy back-paddling to turn the canoe around as the bow paddler settled himself on his knees. The feathers floated out to the left of Duffy as the canoe was being turned, but then suddenly they snagged on something, and the long string of feathers grew taut.

The stern paddler, intent on the turn, gave a strong back pull. Duffy let out a grunt and grabbed his headdress. Too late. He caught one of the buffalo horns just before the whole thing fell in the water. "Stop!" he yelled. The canoe banked to the left. Duffy's sleeve and part of his jacket went underwater as he held to the horn and the snag held too.

Duncan burst out laughing at poor Duffy's predicament. Probably the leather strap the feathers were sewn to had got caught on the wire trap that kept leaves out of the fountain water. It was obvious that Duffy would fall in before he'd let go of his horns.

"Hold on, Duffy, we'll jerk it loose," the bow paddler said. The two paddlers worked in unison, but all they accomplished was to drag anchor farther out from shore. Duncan hoped they hadn't wrecked Mr. Garringer's leaf trap.

"Stop paddling," Duffy said. "I'll just haul it up. It's loose. We've probably messed up the fountain mechanism."

Carefully Duffy gathered up his long train of feathers. "Feels like I've got a fish on the line," he laughed. "Gosh, I hope the horns don't come unglued." He turned his attention briefly to the bulky horns in his lap, setting them gently behind him.

At that moment there came a scream from the stern paddler. "Look! A snake!"

Duncan grinned as he lay on his stomach on the rope-bridge platform, his chin in his hands. Unlikely, he thought. It was possible though. . . . Some curious water snake might come up from the creek to the lake and be attracted by the torches.

A hot argument had sprung up in that canoe as to whether or not a snake had actually been seen. "It was there, Duffy, I tell you. It was as big around as my arm. You'd have seen it too if you hadn't been fussing with your stupid horns."

"What do you mean 'stupid'? They're borrowed from the Y. If they come unglued—"

"Forget the horns. It was a snake, I tell you— Maybe a copperhead."

"So what? Big deal, it's gone now," Duffy said. "Put your paddle down and help me drag this thing overboard. It's not the fountain thing it got snagged on. It's a book satchel."

Duncan felt as if a gong from a terrible iron bell had gone off right at his ear. He was jarred to his feet. He leaped off the platform and fell into a crape-myrtle bush. A huge sob welled up in his throat as he ran toward the shore.

He waded a few steps into the water and stopped, sick at the thought of what would be found there. He wouldn't claim it; they could dispose of it.

"Aaaaaagh!" The canoe rocked vigorously as Duffy leaped backward into the lap of the stern paddler. Poor Duffy. What a gruesome shock to find in that satchel a rotting, six-day-dead soft-shell.

"It just about bit my leg off!" Duffy screamed.

Duncan went limp. He couldn't move.

"I told you, and you wouldn't *believe* me," the stern paddler shouted. "It's what had hold of your feathers, Duffy."

"It bit my leg," Duffy repeated. "If I hadn't had on the leggings. . . ."

Duncan laughed himself silly as he dove into the water to go claim Big Neck. The two other canoes had closed in on each side of Duffy's canoe. The cry was to "Get it out of the boat!" The paddlers, half standing in their jittery canoes, were reaching with their paddles, trying to turn the book satchel over so the straps could be looped over a paddle and the heaving dangerous "snake" dumped overboard before it came out and bit somebody else.

Duncan swam fast and came up between two of the canoes. He pushed his way between them, jumped himself up, and hung over the gunwale of Duffy's canoe. "I'll get it. It's my book satchel," he said, trying to sound calm.

"Look out, you fool. There's a huge snake coiled up in there!" The bow paddler thrust his paddle between Duncan and the book satchel.

"There *is*, Dunc. It bit me." Duffy's hideously painted face gleamed in the yellow torchlight.

"Who's this kid, Duffy? He's nuts."

"No, he isn't. I know him. It's probably his book satchel. He's not afraid of snakes either. Hold that flap down, Dunc. That one bites."

"It's not a snake though, Duffy. I know what's in it. It's a turtle."

His words were drowned out though as the thin-faced "Indian" whom Duffy was sitting on, said hotly, "You *think* you know! But a snake's in it now." He pushed Duffy off his lap and held out his hands half a paddle's length apart. "I saw at least this much of it."

"That was just Big Neck."

"Shoot, yeh. That's a big neck. And with a neck that big, you can guess how big the whole snake is."

"But it's a *turtle*. Big Neck's a soft-shell turtle."

"This guy's out of his cotton-pickin' mind," sputtered the stern paddler.

The argument went wildly back and forth; even those who hadn't seen Big Neck's head had firm opinions on the matter. It ended abruptly when Duncan said, "Please, you guys, let me have him. I need him for the Science Fair. He's my science project, and I thought he was dead."

Now the paddles came to rest across the gunwales, and the canoes were steady again. "Honest, he's a turtle. I'm going to tame him." He explained how Big Neck had gotten into this predicament. Then he held the flap down over the angry eye that peered out, and Duffy helped lift the satchel over the side of the canoe.

The canoes left then, slowly, for their debarkation, under the willow tree. Duncan dragged his precious property through the water to the shore of the island.

The teen-agers watched him bundle it carefully under his arm. "It's only a turtle," one of them said. They began to dance again, barefoot on the grass. Practically unnoticed, Duncan slipped between the dancers, under the lanterns, past the sign: "Trespassers Will Be Mugged."

The Girl in the Peach Tree

Duncan was followed around the lake by a crowd of children begging to see Big Neck. But Duncan was not about to take him out of the book satchel. After all he'd been through, Big Neck deserved a rest. "You can see him at the museum tomorrow," Duncan said for the fifteenth time.

A few children continued to pester him as far as the footbridge across Sugar Creek. Here angrily he turned around and told them to get lost, to quit bugging him, the answer was NO!

"You're mean," the littlest girl pouted, but they left.

"Why are they bugging you, and 'No' *what?*" came a voice from the peach tree by the bridge.

Duncan froze to the ground. It was Paula's voice! The whole peach tree shook as Paula swung on a branch by her knees and dropped off to the grass.

"Why did that girl say you were mean?"

"It's . . . it's just what I've got in here," Duncan stuttered.

"What's in there?" In the glow from the mercury vapor light, Paula's pert face was a shining pale green.

"A soft-shelled turtle," Duncan mumbled.

"Lemme see him."

Without hesitation Duncan put the satchel on the grass, undid the buckles, and turned back the flap.

Paula bent over, her hands on her flower-patched blue-jean knees. Her braids with the yellow ribbons flopped forward, and the little pearl on its gold chain swung like a pendulum. "Oh, gosh, would you look at him. You don't have to take him out all the way, Duncan. I can see him. What are you going to do with him?"

"Take him to the museum."

Paula glanced up at the dark museum on the hill across the creek. "It's locked," she said.

"I know where the key is."

"Can I go with you?"

Duncan had somewhat recovered from the initial shock of having Paula drop out of the peach tree, but now the nervousness returned. What would they talk about? He felt absolutely tongue-tied.

But he soon discovered that talking to Paula was no problem. She was a chatterbox. She asked him a million questions as they walked over the bridge and up the path by the cheetah cage. She wanted

195

all the details about how Big Neck had got into the lake. She giggled at the picture Duncan presented of Van Meyerding and the parachute, but he had a hard time making her understand why he couldn't find Big Neck in the lake.

"The arrow scouts were fiddling with the fountain switch," he told her. "It was off when Big Neck landed, and then it came on again. Naturally I didn't think to look under the fountain."

"Why not?" Paula demanded.

"Because I saw him land in smooth water—that's why."

"You should have seen that the fountain was off."

"Well, I didn't. I was too mad at Van."

At the back door of the museum Paula held the book satchel by its straps while Duncan climbed up on the brick wall and got down the emergency key. He unlocked the basement door and turned on the light.

Upstairs in the Animal Room, Joe the crow rumpled up his feathers and complained at being disturbed. The parrot spoke a ladylike "hello," and Paula replied in the same voice.

Big Neck glared suspiciously at Duncan from under the flaps, but when he tumbled out into the slate pool, he went mad with delight. With his neck out long he raced around the pool, skidding recklessly into other turtles and the two baby alligators. Then he coasted up to a flat rock and rested his chin on it, his legs out loose.

The green male turtle had come fully awake and with his long curved claws began his off-schedule courtship of the big green female.

"Look at that mean little greenie," Paula said indignantly.

Duncan laughed. He didn't feel like explaining all that to Paula. With the empty book satchel over his shoulder, he went to the door and turned out the light. They walked past the dinosaurs and down the basement steps in silence.

When the door was locked and the key returned to its place, Paula said, "I don't see why you keep *bad* turtles in that pool. That mean one was going to scratch that other one's eyes out. Why did you laugh? I thought you liked turtles."

"I do."

"Then why do you laugh when they fight?"

"He wasn't fighting."

"He was too. He was about to—"

"No, he wasn't!" Gosh, what a stubborn girl!

"Duncan McKenna, you know darn well—Hey, I can't see down these steps." Paula reached out and caught Duncan's hand. "You've got owl eyes."

"I . . . I . . . I just know these steps." Holding her hand down the steps had set his heart to racing. He dropped it as soon as they came to the lighted area around the Elephant Rocks. He began to run.

"Don't go so fast. It's creepy in here." He stopped and waited for her. Across the creek the festival was closing down for the night. Only one more day.

"You go ahead and lead me, Duncan." She took his hand again as they walked along the shadowy trail above Sugar Creek.

Being with Paula was nerve-wracking. No sooner had he got used to her, so that he could talk along and argue even, than she'd do something that would get him to feeling feeble again. She could lead herself! She could see as well as he could! But he didn't drop her hand.

"You know that creepy voice you had. I found out how you did it."

"You did?"

"It was helium, wasn't it?"

She kept up a stream of chatter as he led her through the woods. At the steep bank he let go of her hand. "You have to run to get up here. Grab the trees."

"I know. I've done it lots of times." But when she was almost at the top, she slid back a little. "The rock's gone."

"We dug it up."

"What for? It was my favorite rock."

"Mine too."

"You've ruined this shortcut. What'd you do with it?"

"Built a waterfall."

Now Paula began asking questions about the waterfall and the rocks in his collection. He finally got in a question himself. "What were you doing in the peach tree?"

"Waiting."

"Waiting for what?"

"Oh, just waiting."

She might have been waiting for Steve and his guitar. After a moment when she didn't say anything, he said, "Steve sounds pretty good on the microphone, doesn't he?"

"He ought to learn something besides that one song. Anyway that turtle was more interesting."

Duncan wasn't absolutely sure that she meant what he thought she meant by that remark, but it gave him a positively giddy feeling inside. He jumped up and caught a limb of a hickory tree.

"The pet show's tomorrow," Paula said.

"It's not a pet show. It's a dog-training show."

"I know it. That new leash law's a gyp."

"Say, Paula, did you hear about those Afghan dogs me and Louie saw on the paper route?"

"Last year I saw 'em at the park. Same ones."

"You did? When? What time of day was it?"

It was in the afternoon, Paula said, that she saw the old man, and he had only three dogs with him. Two were black, and one was white, and the old man was wearing saddle shoes and an orange jacket with a flowered necktie.

"That's not the same one."

"Yes, it is. He had a beard."

"Lots of people have beards. How big was he?"

"About like Mr. Garringer. I patted the dogs."

Duncan shook his head. "The one I saw with

Louie was huge. And he wore army stuff, and he's a hermit—he doesn't like people. He was supposed to come for the dog training, but he won't do it."

"I bet it's the same man," Paula said. "The dogs had curly hair and curly tails."

"Poodles," Duncan said.

"No, Duncan. Poodles are little."

"Not all of them. Some are big."

"But I said 'curly tails.' Poodles are clipped with a bunch of fur at the ends."

Paula was really a stubborn girl. But it was fun to argue with her. She finally said she had to go home, and ran up Princeton Avenue.

Duncan continued down Sterling. He wished now for another reason that the hermit would finally show up at the Festival. Then he could prove to Paula he was right—this wasn't the same man she had seen in a flowered tie. But the irony of that was obvious. If the hermit *did* come tomorrow, he wouldn't be around to win his argument with Paula. He'd be racing home for his bicycle!

The Confrontation

Today, Sunday the eighteenth of September, would be noted on Duncan's project report as the first day in the training of the notorious *Trionyx Spiniferus,* otherwise known as Big Neck. As soon as he finished lunch Duncan turned on the faucet at the back of the house and ran to the pool to see his waterfall in action for the first time. Water gurgled into the cave of the geode, washing the pink crystals and overflowing down the side of the mountain, bringing out the color and sparkle of the rocks —banded granite, amythyst quartz, spotted leopardite—down to the broad base, the black pitted favorite rock. He leaned over and took a drink from the lip where the stream spilled out of the cave. It had a plasticky taste. But that would clear up when the pipe was thoroughly rinsed.

Before putting Big Neck in the pool, he'd wash away the taste of cement too, drain it a few times, and partially fill it with sand. He was rubbing off the cement spills from the rocks with his thumb when the gate clanked open and Gates Lee burst into the backyard. "He's there!" he gasped.

Duncan whirled around as if he'd been shot with the hose. "He *is?*"

"Come on, quick, Dunc!"

Duncan's father came out the back door. "Who's over there that's so exciting, Gates? You boys aren't planning a collision with the Van Meyerding gang, are you?"

"Nuh-uh. No, sir." Gates backed into the low branches of the apple tree. "It's just—it's just that it's the last day, and, uh, they've got that school they're having you know, for teaching you how to train your dog. . . ."

Gates obviously wasn't sure if he ought to bring up the hermit. Duncan interrupted, "Hey, Gates, is that crazy hermit and the dogs over there?"

Gates spit out a leaf he'd been chewing on and grinned with great relief, his front teeth gleaming. "Yeh, he's there. Come on if you want to see him." He chinned himself on an apple tree bough.

"You go. I'll meet you . . . you know. . . ." Duncan ran into the house, his brain in a whirl. He'd almost given up hope that the hermit would come. Early this morning he and Louie had done the paper route together for the second time. It seemed much more than a week ago that Duncan had had his terrifying backward glance at the hermit. The memory sent a shiver of excitement over him.

Let's see . . . he might need something to quiet the dogs . . . just in case. . . . He got out a package of Tony's frozen fish heads. And he'd made that stupid promise, so he'd better call. . . .

In his pocket was the dime and the card Joey had given him. His mother was taking a shower and his father was in the backyard, so he'd save the dime.

Quickly he dialed the second number on the card. A lady answered the phone, and he asked for Joey. He could hear her say, "Banks, somebody wants to speak to Joey." After a minute Joey came on, and Duncan told him that the hermit was in the park and that he had remembered his promise to call.

Joey was happy he'd called. He said he knew Duncan would keep his promise, and he told Duncan to please pat the puppies through the wire and say, "Joey's thinkin' about you."

Duncan said okay and hung up, feeling slightly foolish. It was hard to believe that Joey could be as simple-minded as he was and still hold down a job at the TV station.

Marshall, Monroe, Steve, and Gates were already at Louie's house when Duncan arrived. As they sped down Maryland Avenue to East Boulevard, Steve told how he had seen the hermit at exactly 2:01 by his watch. He had four dogs with him and was making the turn around the lake under the willow tree.

They followed the paper route out to its end and

beyond to the broad dirt path. At the rise in the land they got off their bikes. Here Monroe was supposed to hide in the sumac as a lookout. Gates had agreed to be an advance lookout back at the edge of the woods. But neither of them wanted to stand guard yet. They wanted at least to see the place. So, all six boys continued down the path pushing their bicycles, sniffing the air for the smell of the untidy dog pen.

The wind was wrong. The dogs scented them first. They yipped a few times, and then let forth a mighty chorus of howls. From the broken tar road you could see them, a row of shaggy chests and floppy ears, all sizes and colors standing on their hind legs at the fence.

Monroe wanted to run across the slanting bridge, but Louie caught him by the arm and told him sternly to get to his post. "And, Gates, you too. Go back up Randolph Road to that dense thicket. Hide in the woods and signal Monroe with an owl hoot if you see the old guy coming."

Steve checked his watch. "We shouldn't cut it too close. The way I figure it, he's finished the park and is heading on back. That gives us ten minutes about. I say we get busy and scram out of here in five minutes, to be safe. He'll hear the dogs way back there and speed up."

Duncan handed the bag of thawing fish heads to Marshall and pointed to the dog pen down the bank and across the creek. "Go feed these to the dogs, Marsh. See if you can calm 'em down. You can wade across; the creek's shallow." Then with Louie and Steve, Duncan ran across the tilted bridge and down to the shack.

Steve examined the many doors of the shack while Duncan and Louie pawed through the undergrowth at the base of the slanting concrete bridge support from which Duncan had tumbled. No luck. They even looked under the old rubber tire that Duncan had stumbled over, but there were no white envelopes anywhere.

Marshall was having no success with the dogs either. They ate the fish heads but kept on barking.

"This is stupid," Louie said, pulling at his ear. "If Gates *did* see him coming, we'd never hear the signal with that racket."

Duncan was ready to give up too. He should never have thought the old hermit was such a half-wit that he wouldn't have even noticed the four envelopes spilled in his front yard. He had probably already bought dog food with the money.

Duncan whistled and beckoned to Marshall who tossed the rest of the fish heads over the fence and began to run back across the creek as if *the signal* had come. But Steve, after a glance at his watch as he, Louie, and Duncan ran up the path to the bridge, said there were still a couple of safe minutes left, and he wanted to take a look in the window.

Louie glanced apprehensively at Duncan over the top of his knuckles as he bit his fingernails, but he didn't argue.

Steve crawled out on the slanting abutment and lay down, his neck stretched out toward the window. His black-rimmed glasses no longer slipped down his nose; he had tied a rubber band around the loose hinges.

"I see the gun!" he whispered hoarsely. "Hey, he's got some papers, too. Yes, it's envelopes. I bet it's the money. Go on down there, Dunc."

Duncan climbed over the bridge railing and dropped to the sandy shore. It was an exhilarating thought that here on the verge of failure, in the last two minutes of the search, the money might be found. A less exhilarating second thought also entered his mind: to walk into that house was some sort of a crime.

His hand was on the latch when Louie called down the bank. Monroe was jumping up and down beside Louie, shaking his hands. "Hey, come on quick, you guys. Monroe says there's a car out there with a man in it."

Steve craned his neck around. "Not the hermit?"

"No, but the car's parked at the path."

Steve glanced at his watch again. "I'm sure it's Louie's money, Dunc. There's handwriting on the envelope—like just a name, no stamp or anything."

That was the way the envelopes had looked, all right. Duncan pushed the door open. Standing on the bare plank floor of the shack, his heart in an uproar, Duncan had the feeling that the old black pot-bellied stove on its four clawed feet, glared with its three triangular eyes and would have blasted him out of there if it could have. But Steve was telling him where to look . . . on a shelf over a calendar.

He'd have stepped on the bed and reached up for the envelopes except that Louie appeared, wild-eyed, and grabbed his elbow. Monroe, pale and whining, "He's coming, he's coming," hopped around in the background.

"I *told* you we wouldn't hear Gates when he hooted," Louie said, his voice shaking. "He's there now, talking to the man in the car. We'll have to scram across the pasture. We can't meet him on the path!"

Duncan stumbled backward as Louie dragged him out the door. "Wait, Louie, it might be better just to *meet* him on the path. Make it look like we took a wrong turn—we thought it was a shortcut to Eastover. We can't push our bikes through that field."

Louie shook his head. "We have to. He'd recognize us, Dunc, and you can't tell what a lunatic'll do!"

Monroe, with a tourniquet hold on Louie's arm, kept up a steady wail: "Ooooh, gee, what'll we do? He knows we're here, he knows we're here. His dogs were smelling Gates's bike in the woods, and now they're choking their necks to get at us! They'll tear us apart. They'd have already done it except for the man in the car."

Steve, who had dropped off his spying perch, barged in between Louie and Monroe. "Shut up, Monroe," he said roughly. "Don't crack up now."

Marshall was frantically beckoning from the top of the high bank across the creek. *That* would be the quickest way to the bikes. They skimmed over the water, bringing on a louder clamor from the dogs in the pen.

A superagility seemed to lift them up over the steep cliff full of bird holes to the old road. They skidded to a halt as over the brow of the high place in the path came the old man with Monroe's bicycle in hand. His enormous sandy-gray beard brushed the seat of the bicycle as he strode brusquely along.

What? It wasn't an optical illusion! The coat that barreled around the old man was *orange!* Dull and dusty, but *orange.* And on his feet were dusty mis-shapen *saddle shoes.* Duncan felt double-crossed.

The hermit blustered to a halt in front of Marshall, who stood behind his bicycle as if prepared to use it defensively, his face set in a scholarly scowl. "What in tarnation d'ya think you're doin' on my property?" the old man demanded.

Duncan, in a tight huddle with Monroe, Louie and Steve, had been so thunderstruck by the shock-ing spectacle of the World War I veteran that had crystallized in his imagination in an orange sport coat and saddle shoes, that he hadn't until now even looked at the four long-legged hairy dogs or the man in a dark suit who held their taut leashes.

The dogs stood barking fiercely, two on each side of their master. The hermit's voice was drowned out as he whirled around to stab a finger toward the edge of the thicket on Randolph Road, Gates's sentry position. Out in the field was a small figure, Gates, approaching slowly through the sumac and goldenrod.

The old man whirled on the dogs then. "Shoooosh!" he roared.

Instantly they hushed. In unison their long muzzles turned to watch Gates's cautious advance through the underbrush. Two were the color of the beard, a yellowish white, with dark faces. One was dark red and the fourth, a bluish black. Except for their dripping, twitching tongues, they stood motionless like statues, aloof and dignified. But on top of their heads a ridiculous confusion of fine silky hair sprouted forth. Long wavy hair trailed off their ears and flowed down over their deep chests. Like the chaps worn by cowboys this silky bush fluffed out on their legs and made them look tremendous. Surprisingly their backs were so downy their hip bones showed, and their curving tails were featherless.

Marshall, gripping the handles of his bicycle, cleared his throat. "Er . . . ah . . . you've got some unusual dogs here, sir," he said in his low nasal drawl.

"Don't gimme any smart runaround, young feller. I don't like sneakin', spyin' butt-ins. Uh *huh!* Thought so!" He aimed a finger at Louie and then at Duncan. "*You* two." He bristled around to the man in the suit, standing behind him. "*Them* two was here before, prowlin' around."

As the bushy beard jerked aside, Duncan saw what was under it—a broad, gaudy, flowered necktie! He might have expected it. He had a brief mental image of the victorious Paula, flipping her long brown hair back over her shoulder, saying "I knew I was right, Duncan. You and Louie were so scared you couldn't see straight." He wasn't any seven feet tall either, Duncan noted.

"You boys come with me," the old man commanded. "And *you* there," he said to the man, "bring those dogs up ahead."

The man obligingly let the dogs drag him up on the bridge. Roughly the hermit bumped Monroe's rattly bicycle across the gap between the road and the bridge.

Monroe frantically jerked at his sweat shirt, stretching it down over his knees. In a small high voice he protested, "That's my bicycle, sir."

"So?"

Monroe's face was bright pink under smears of dirt. "He's stealing it. He's stealing it," he muttered.

Louie put his arm around Monroe's shoulders and said softly, "We'll get it back, Monroe."

The man in the dark suit was asking the hermit

about puppies he had for sale; it seemed to have a calming effect. But when the shack came in view with its door hanging open as Duncan had left it, the hermit flared up angrily. With the back of his hand he hit the man on the shoulder and pointed a shaking finger at the boys, lagging along behind.

"Just as I figured! Busted into my dadburn place, they did. Got a mind to—" He began running down the path. He left Monroe's bicycle on its side with the wheels spinning, and bolted into the shack.

The man with the dogs arrived just as the old man stalked out the door with a gun in his hand. "Here, you take the dogs," the man said, dropping the leashes over the hermit's arm. Then, grasping the gun firmly by the barrel, he said, "Oh, *ho*, I see you've got a Springfield '03. Well, well, been a long time since I've handled one of these. Glad you brought it out. Old World War I rifle. My grandfather had one of these up over the mantel back home." His voice was loud and jovial.

The dogs' leashes had dropped to the ground. The hermit bent over to pick them up. "It's a Springfield, all right," he grumbled through his shimmering bush, "but it ain't a 30-06 like you think. It's a .22 target rifle."

The man took the clip out and opened the bolt. A cartridge flipped out on the ground. "So I see, so I see. What do you shoot around here? Rabbits?"

"No, rats." The old man cocked his head on a slant and the beard jutted off to the side, exposing the flowered necktie. "You figure I might fire off at the boys, eh?"

"Not at all, sir. I didn't give it a thought—just admired your Springfield. It handles nice, a well-balanced gun." He sighted down the barrel.

"You don't fool me, mister, but I'll tell you now I ain't that loony." He tapped the side of his head. "I've got my ways o' dealin' with a pesky youngun. First thing they'll set their hand to is that there gun. Next thing you know they blow theirselves up with it." He jerked his thumb up toward the boys on the road, and the shrillness of his voice faded, so that his words couldn't be heard.

Gates came up then, panting from working his way through the overgrown field. "What's going on? Who's that other man?"

"A customer," Louie said. "He's going to buy a puppy."

"Oh, oh, he's got Monroe's bike down there."

"He stole it," Monroe muttered.

"Why didn't you beat it when I signaled?"

"We couldn't hear you with the dogs barking. And we never did find the money," Louie said.

The conversation between the man and the hermit seemed endless. Monroe kept mumbling, "What's he gonna do with my bike?"

"See them holes?" The hermit pointed to the steep bank across the creek. "Rats! I hate 'em."

The man picked up the cartridge that had fallen on the ground and put the clip back in the gun.

Then, as if they'd forgotten the boys waiting on the bridge, the two men headed for the dog pen.

The four dogs were returned to the pen, and a puppy was brought out. It struggled like a bucking pony foal and got its big front paws tangled in the old man's beard. He reared his chin back, freeing the beard. The puppy licked him in the face as he carried it over to a wooden box where he sat down.

With a rope tied loosely around the puppy's neck, he made it stand like a show dog. He was apparently telling the man how long the hair would grow on different parts of the body as his hand patted around where the heavy feathering was on the big dogs.

"Wish we could go see that puppy," Gates said. "Do you think he'd mind?"

"Would he!" Steve's blond hair stood up in peaks on each side giving him a wise-eyed owl look. "You didn't hear all the things he called us. He thinks we were going to steal his gun. I think he's got Louie's money in there too. I saw the whole place through the window, and there were papers up on a shelf."

"Why do we have to wait? Let's get out of here," Monroe said. "Now's a good time to sneak in there and get my bike. Come on, Dunc. It's your fault we're here. You go get it."

It *was* a good time, while the hermit was busy with the customer. Cautiously Duncan crawled down the bushy bank behind the shack, holding back on rocks and the strong roots of sumac so as to make a minimum of noise. With his eye on the hermit he soundlessly picked up Monroe's bicycle. But in backing it around, he bumped into the rubber tire and the back fender rattled.

"Hold on there," the hermit roared. "Put down that blame bicycle! I'm not through with you yet." And with that, he came with giant strides along the gravel shore, the gun in one hand, the beard fanning down from his ruddy face. The customer followed, the pup in his arms.

With his heart beating a din in his ears, Duncan laid the bicycle down, accidentally flattening the bulb of Monroe's horn. It let out a squawk.

"Come down here, all of you," thundered the hermit at the boys huddled by the bridge.

Monroe was pale again; he had Steve by the wrist. They started to climb down the bank, but the hermit bellowed at them again to come by the path. What did they want to do? Ruin his windbreak? "Got no use for a vandalizin' snoopin' youngun. Served you right you lost your dadblame money. Now, here you come back again, bustin' in like you had a right . . ."

"You found it? Can I have it?" Duncan blurted.

"Dang if I think you deserve it, bustin' in like this. How'd I know what else you might of took, if I hadn't caught you before you took it? Didn't think the old man could git around so fast, eh?" He squinted at the boys who had come up on both sides of Duncan. The rifle lay over his arm.

"We didn't come to steal anything—"

The old man grabbed his beard in his hand and

fixed Louie with a fierce glare. "Caught you spyin', hate a snooper."

"We didn't—" Gates and Steve jabbed Monroe before he could say any more.

"Er . . . ah . . . I think there's a misunderstanding here, sir," Marshall drawled.

"Can I have my bicycle?"

"Shooosh!" Monroe shrank behind Duncan as if he'd been hit by a hot blast.

Then Louie tried again, meekly. "We-we-we sort of got lost the first time, sir."

"Lost, eh. And then you make it your business to spy in my windows."

"We didn't mean—"

Monroe pinched the skin over Duncan's shoulder blades as the hermit stabbed a finger at him and roared, "Ha! You *didn't mean*. Of course you meant it, and now you come sneakin' back again. Why, I could charge you with breakin' and enterin'. How would you like for your pa to have to go and git you out of jail? Why, you might of stole my gun if I hadn't caught you red-handed."

"No, we wouldn't. We just came back to look for the money I lost."

"You lost it while you were spyin'. Served you right. Why else didn't you come straight out and ask for it? I've got a mind to turn you all in to the police. . . ."

Duncan had had lectures at home and at school before, but never anything like this. It was painful to have to look into the blazing eyes of the old man.

For relief he glanced past the hermit, across the creek to the high clay bank full of kingfisher holes. A flicker of motion caught his eye. A familiar, blood-tingling, ugly shape whizzed from one hole on the bank to another—that was no bird, no kingfisher! "A rat!" he whispered.

The word clipped off the old man's tirade. He spun around and sat down on the ground, his feet crossed, elbows braced on his knees, the gunstock at his shoulder. "Where?"

"There! It went into that hole on the bank about a foot down from the top, left of those dead roots."

Every eye followed the aim of the gun to the bank across the creek, the bank that twice before Duncan had sailed up like a frightened deer.

Monroe had a squeeze on Duncan's arm again. You could hear the tick of Steve's watch and the heavy breathing of the pup asleep in the man's arms.

Then, yes! Sun glittered on the sleek hide of a big gray rat! The .22 sang out—a high ping. The rat leaped in the air and rolled down the red clay bank. "Filthy dang varmint!" the hermit exclaimed and spat on the ground. A smile split the bushy beard in two.

"You got him!" Monroe jumped up and clapped his hands.

"Never miss." The old man smoothed down the beard and ejected the empty shell.

Monroe began to run, but Louie caught him by

the arm. "Is it all right if we go look at him?" Monroe asked.

"Fetch it here," the hermit commanded.

It was a relief to let loose and run. Duncan had begun to prickle all over; the water felt good as they splashed through it. Whew! Never before in his life had Duncan been grateful for a rat. It lay where it had fallen, dead as a rock. Monroe wanted to take it home and stuff it, to scare people with.

"It's too beat up," Gates said. "Its neck is bleeding."

"Yekkkkk!" Louie grabbed his face with both hands. "Repulsive."

"You could patch that up," Steve said, "but Monroe's no taxidermist. If you don't do it right, they stink."

Duncan and Marshall knew what they'd do with the rat, though, and they grinned at each other. They'd take it home to the museum's black rat snake. It had learned to eat dead meat if it was still warm. Duncan took the rat by the tail, and they walked back through the water.

"Can I have it to feed a snake at the Nature Museum?" he asked the hermit.

"Why in thunder didn't you come up like that and ask for the money you lost, 'stead of"—he waved his hand through the air—"Aw, skip it. Yes, keep the dang varmint."

The old man went into the shack and came out with the four envelopes that had slid out of Dun-

218

can's pocket a week ago. He gave them to Duncan. "And take your bike out of here too." He gave Monroe's front tire a light kick.

"Yes, sir." Monroe let out a noisy sigh. "Thanks a lot. Whew! I'm glad you're not mad anymore."

Everyone glared at Monroe who never knew when to shut up.

The long-legged puppy lay in the man's arms, its muzzle snuggled under his ear. Duncan put the rat on the ground and patted the puppy. "He likes you. He's gone to sleep."

The man smiled. "I've been standing here so long with him in my arms we've gotten to be pretty good friends."

As Duncan patted the puppy's soft stomach, he had the strangest feeling that he'd been here in this same situation before, talking to this same man. It was an eerie feeling that couldn't really be a memory at all.

He asked if the man was going to buy the puppy, and the man said he wasn't sure he could afford such an aristocratic dog. Then suddenly it came to Duncan what had been familiar about the situation. It was that sentence, the one about the man's having stood there so long with the dog in his arms that they'd gotten to be pretty good friends. It was just last Wednesday that Joey the Clown had said something like that about the pine snake: "I've been sittin' here so long with him we've gotten to be pretty good buddies."

The hermit went into the shack, and the boys all crowded around to play with the puppy. "I know who you are," Gates said, grinning up at the man. "You've got a WSOC-TV sticker on your car, and I've seen you doing the news."

"That's right. I'm Banks Linden."

"Only on TV you wear glasses," Steve said. "Hey, look, this dog's ear is a whole octave long." He measured the ear.

Now Duncan remembered why the man looked familiar. But there was somewhere else he had seen him, he thought, besides reading the news on TV. "Do you ever come over to the Nature Museum?" he asked. "Do you know my father? He's the director of it."

"Sure I know Dave McKenna. He comes out to the studio every week or so."

"To be on 'The Joey Show,'" Duncan said.

"Yes."

As Duncan looked up at Banks Linden, that "something familiar'" bolted into perspective. He noticed a pattern of fine lines fanning out from the corners of Banks Linden's blue-green eyes, and in that instant the pieces of the puzzle fell into place. He almost burst out with, Oh, you're Joey the Clown! but something held him back, something kept him from saying it.

It seemed foolish, but it was like a secret pledge between himself and Joey. At least for now he

would pretend, as Joey would and as apparently Banks Linden liked to pretend, to keep the newscaster and the clown separate. It was almost supernatural to think of this man and Joey as one person. It was as if Duncan had had a caterpillar that had turned into a butterfly and then when he was ready to let it go, there in the jar was the caterpillar again, chomping on a green leaf.

It was more fun to let Joey keep his own special integrity. Duncan thought of the stubbly face and the big white mouth with the red-painted nose, the simple-minded Joey, who was so solidly just Joey that you forgot that he had to be somebody else when he wasn't dressed in his swallowtail coat and the hat with the wobbly flower. What had happened, Duncan figured, was that the "somebody else" —Banks Linden—leaning on the railing of the cattle barn in his Joey clothes, had worried when Duncan had spilled out the story of a crazy old man with fierce dogs and a gun, and the plan of a bunch of boys to sneak up on the place. Duncan had trusted Joey, though, so Banks Linden couldn't let Joey down by botching up the plan. He was trapped in his Joey skin. He couldn't make sensible suggestions. He had to do it Joey's way. And then when the phone call came, he split into two people: one who stayed home and dreamed about patting some silky-haired dogs and the other who got in his car and went to see about buying an Afghan pup just to be there as a buffer between the boys and the old eccentric.

What might have happened without him? Duncan wondered. They'd never know.

Monroe, smiling dimples into his baby face, asked Banks Linden if he knew Joey the Clown.

"As a matter of fact, he's a very close friend of mine," Banks Linden said, winking at Duncan.

"Ha-ha, he's a nut," Monroe said, hugging the puppy.

"Monroe still watches 'The Joey Show,'" Steve teased.

"Aw, I do not," Monroe protested. "He's always got a lot of nutty little kids on his program."

Marshall coughed importantly. "And a few, er—ah—*famous* adults like Duncan's father."

Banks Linden laughed. "Right, he's a pretty famous fellow."

The hermit came out of the shack with a dishpan full of kibbled dog food and said for them to "git," he had work to do. And did or didn't Mr. Linden want to buy the pup?

Mr. Linden said he'd have to talk it over with his wife. The price was somewhat steeper than he had expected, but he could tell by the way the puppy took to the boys that it would survive his young son's affection.

Marshall picked up the rat. "Come on, you all. We've got to hurry before this rat gets stiff."

On the way down the path Duncan took out of

his pocket the card with Joey's name on it and the dime. "I owe Joey the Clown a dime," he said to Banks Linden. "Would you give it to him when you see him, and tell him thanks but I didn't need it."

Banks Linden said he'd be glad to. The card, Duncan put carefully back in his pocket. He'd keep it and those telephone numbers in case he should ever need them again.